Two Girls
from
Nazareth

JUDY BARNES

ISBN 978-1-953223-45-6 (paperback)
ISBN 978-1-953223-44-9 (digital)

Rushmore Press LLC
1 800 460 9188
www.rushmorepress.com

Printed in the United States of America

FOREWORD

A long time ago in a faraway land two little girls were born to different families. These girls were like sisters. They played with each other and continued to be best friends into their teens. Both of the girls were named Mary and grew up hoping to be the mother of the long awaited Messiah, although it seemed unlikely. He was to be born in Bethlehem and neither of the girls had ever even visited the small village not far from Jerusalem. They had never even visited Jerusalem. They were both of the right lineage, however, and so were any number of Mary's throughout Israel. They had heard that the Prophets of ancient times had said he would be a Nazarene. They both lived in Nazareth, but then so did many other girls named Mary.

Writing a book about the birth of the Christ Child was not an easy task. Nothing much is said about Mary and Joseph before his birth. Nothing much is said about Mary and Joseph after his birth. There are a lot of scriptural references about the coming of the Messiah, however, very little about his earthly parents. I thought it would be interesting to have a little bit of background, although fictional, as to the personalities of Mary and Joseph up until the time of Jesus' birth.

Although this is mostly a fictional story, I thought it would be interesting to give the main characters personality and charisma.

IN MEMORIUM
Lucy Bradford
1945-2004

Lucy Bradford was a good friend to me. She was so much help to me in critiquing this novel. Her thoughts and additions and deletions were invaluable to me. I would have had a much more difficult time writing this book without her help. She has stood behind me as a friend and critic throughout this whole endeavor.

There were others who read this manuscript in its infant state and I thank each one of them also. I don't want to name names for fear of leaving someone out. But be sure to know how much I love each and every one of you.

In 2004 Lucy died of cancer. I miss her very much.

CHAPTER
ONE

The sun was lowering in the western sky and gave promise that tomorrow should be a beautiful day. It was important that tomorrow be perfect. It would not do at all if it should rain. Not on that special day which would be only one of many special days to come.

The red glow on the surrounding hills cast a beauty that was breathtaking from its darkest crimson to its most brilliant pink hues.

The sky was ablaze with, lavender and blue and the sun looked like a large orange ball slowly sinking to its final resting place. While at the same time the moon was peaking just over the top of a hill on the other side of the sky. It was a full moon; harvest time. This is a time of plenty, a time to give thanks to Jehovah for the blessings of life.

Mary Elizabeth sat on top of her favorite rock basking in the splendor of the moment. She was in awe of the resplendent view. She had seen the sun set many times before, however, this moment seemed more unique than anytime she could remember. It was hard for her take her eyes off of the brilliant scene and come back to what was prevalent in her mind.

She knew that her father and brother would soon be home for the evening meal. They work very hard and, although, they had had a large mid-day meal, they were always ravenous by the time they returned in the evening. It was hard work trying to keep the sheep where they belonged and away from other sheep that belonged to neighbors. And herding them back into the pens at night was a real chore. If it were not for the dog, they probably would have to chase the sheep longer. He was a good dog; obedient and faithful.

The girl was well aware that her father did not like to wait for his supper. However, she also knew she could not wait very much longer to talk to Mary; she had been waiting all day. The excitement was getting the best of her. How could she return home without telling the wonderful story of the night's happenings? Her heart seemed to flutter every time she thought about it.

Would Mary never return home? It had been a long day. She had been gone before Mary Elizabeth had finished her chores early this morning. It seemed as though the anxious girl had been back and forth to Mary's house a million times that day waiting impatiently to tell her confidant the good news that she had forced herself to keep inside. Mary was her best friend. She could not tell anyone before she told Mary.

昊昊

Mary was a very common name in Israel. It was told by the Prophets of old, that the Messiah would be born of a virgin named Mary. It seemed like every family had at least one Mary in it and sometimes mere changing only the middle name, hoping that one of their daughters would be 'The Chosen One'. The two girls had 'day dreamed' and discussed how glorious it would be to be the mother of the 'Holy One'. Mary, however, was meek and would not believe that such a thing was possible in her life or even perhaps in her lifetime. Mary Elizabeth, on the other hand, felt quite confident that either of the girls was a good candidate…if the occasion should present itself. It had been many centuries since the prophecy had been foretold.

Many people had already forgotten about the Messiah, God's 'Only Begotten'. Who knew if there would be a Son of God who would take upon him flesh and blood to rule in righteousness? The Romans had ruled so long. No one alive could remember when the Romans were not around.

As she looked over the sleepy village Mary Elizabeth saw a dim light in Mary's window.

[Finally, she is home], she thought to herself, [I cannot wait to tell her.]

With all of her natural enthusiasm, she ran to her best friend's house in anticipation of sharing with Mary her innermost thoughts.

ে০৫

Mary Elizabeth had always had a natural exuberance for life that was exhibited quite often. She had a way of making her presence known. She was boisterous in her conversations; sometimes she laughed a little too loud, and when she cried, she actually wailed. Even at her tender age, she was often used when someone died because she could wail so loud.

Certain women were always called on to be mourners. The louder they could wail the better. Mary Elizabeth was one of these. At times it was embarrassing to listen to her, but Mary never seemed to mind. She always loved Mary Elizabeth for the way she was. She wished she could be more like her. But that was not her nature.

Mary had always been a happy girl, but did not display her feelings quite to the extent that Mary Elizabeth did. Mary's moods were more subdued. She seemed to be able to keep her emotions under wrap a little bit better. Her emotions were evident at given times, but she just did not show it as ecstatically as her best friend did.

Girls were not expected to be outgoing. They were meant to be more like Mary, reserved, quiet, and most of all obedient. Men normally did not like a woman who was domineering or demonstrative, unless the man was somewhat timid, who then was usually called something less than a man, such as a mouse. However, there are exceptions to every rule.

It was the man who was to be unrestrained and overbearing. It was his place to keep the woman and children in line, not the other way around. Mothers were to love and nurture and the father to discipline and keep order.

Mary Elizabeth loved Mary as a sister, but she wished that she would stand up for herself more when it was necessary, as *she* did. But then, their personalities were very compatible. If something needed to be said to someone and Mary was not able to do so, Mary

Elizabeth would step in when called upon. When things were getting intolerable and peace needed to be kept, Mary would make sure that her companion watched what she said. However, when the girls were together, they expressed themselves openly and enjoyed the freedoms their friendship afforded. That is almost certainly the reason they enjoyed each other's company so much.

Mary Elizabeth had an effervescent personality. She had a noticeable twinkle in her eyes and she bubbled every time she spoke which naturally drew people to her instantly. Everybody liked her. The girl had numerous friends, but her best friend was Mary. There was no doubt about that.

Finally, Mary had returned.

Mary Elizabeth ran to her friend's house and was about to burst as she called out, "Mary, please come out, just for a moment, I have something important to tell you!"

She pounded on the door heavily to get the girl's attention. There was no response immediately so Mary Elizabeth pounded even harder. She felt as if her hand was going to shatter like a piece of glass.

Mary appeared at the door opening. "Mary Elizabeth", Mary said harshly, "My mother and I just returned from the market at Sappora. It has been an exhausting day and it is time to prepare supper. I must help Mother. Could we possibly talk after supper?"

≈∞≈

Sappora is a village, not too far from Nazareth on the main highway, and sometimes women would get a better variety of goods or at least a different variety there at a better price. If one could not find what they wanted at the local markets, the trip would be made to another village by mule and wagon to buy what the local markets were lacking. Sometimes they would not find it there, either, but there was always something wonderful that could be bought. It is amazing how someone might go to Sappora for fresh fruit and come back with cloth for a new dress instead, or shop for incense and return with a big, beautiful fish for dinner.

4

The trip would take most of the day because the women would not pay the first price that was asked for an item. They might look at, let us say, a pomegranate. The woman would pick it up, look it over carefully and then quickly put it back down without looking at the merchant at all.

The merchant would keep a keen eye on the purchaser for some sign of expression to try to assess what the buyer was thinking. Then he would pick up the fruit and say, perhaps, "This is one fine pomegranate. I just received a few this morning from Persia." (He probably had a whole wagon load, and certainly not from Persia. They were more likely bought the day before from a local grower. Although, this sounds like lying, they each knew what the other was doing. The purchaser wanted the item at a much lower price than what was reasonable and the merchant wanted to sell the item for more than it was worth. There was really no deception on either part.)

Then he would continue, "You could not find a finer selection of pomegranates anywhere around."

The woman would then pick it up again and look it over again and say, "What is your price?"

Then the merchant would tell the price and the woman would say, "No, too much. Look here, I see a bruise starting right there", pointing to an imaginary spot.

The merchant would then take the pomegranate and examine it for the beginning of a bruise or blemish and although he could find nothing, he would give the woman another price. If the price was acceptable the woman might take several, if not, she would put the pomegranate down and go to another item without reservation.

It was a game that was always enjoyed between the merchant and the purchaser. It was expected.

☜∘☞

"It will only take a moment. I am going to lose my mind if I have to wait another minute before telling you. It is more exciting than you can imagine", Mary Elizabeth bubbled.

"All right, but just a minute", Mary consented, "Mother will have my hide if she must do everything herself."

⊱•⊰

Mary has an older brother named Thomas and an older sister named Mary Saphronia. For some unknown reason, her mother had not been able to conceive after Mary's birth. In fact, her mother had had such a difficult inception, it would have not been surprising if Mary had not been born at all.

Then, after the rough time carrying the baby, Naomi had a long and tedious labor. Mary had been born buttocks first instead of head first like a normal baby. Naomi's recovery had taken many months. At first, it was thought that Naomi might bleed to death. The Midwife had spent more time at Naomi's house than her own. Of course, there were other women who came to relieve her in the evening so she could rest or at times when she had to help another baby come into the world.

The husband could not help because this was of a personal nature and it would not be proper. And he would be terribly embarrassed. A man never helped with the birth; that was the woman's area of expertise. Female problems were not to be dealt with by a man. However, many women were invited.

The women attending the mother-to-be helped to ease the labor by opening all the doors, drawers, and chests in the house. They also untied all knots, ties, and buttons. They placed the key of the Synagogue in the woman's hand and sometimes a Torah pointer as well. All these things were to encourage the womb to open easily.

Someone usually read the first book of Samuel, too, because it tells of Hannah's joy in having Samuel, after years of barrenness.

As soon as the baby was born, even before it was washed, the women each took turns hugging and kissing the baby. Then the midwife sprinkled salt on the baby to protect it from evil spirits and washed it in warm water. She anointed the baby with warm olive oil and powdered it with powder made from ground myrtle leaves. After this, the mid-wife swaddled the baby, to keep the baby tight in

6

a blanket. This was meant to keep the baby snug like it was in the womb and to make the legs grow straight.

Mary Elizabeth's mother, Theresa, had cared for Mary because Naomi was too weak. It was like having twins. The two girls were close because they started out life about the same time with Theresa feeding both. Theresa was a second mother to Mary.

When Mary was about six months old, Naomi was finally strong enough to care for the infant herself, but because she no longer could nurse the child, Theresa continued feeding both girls until they were weaned.

Mary had been conceived when Jacob and Naomi had been married about sixteen years. She had been quite a surprise to everyone in the village. Young Thomas was fourteen years old and her older sister Mary Saphronia was twelve. People were beginning to think the couple would never have other children.

Mary had been a small, sickly baby from the beginning. The Elders said that Jehovah must have had a purpose for her because, by all standards, she should not have survived and neither should have Naomi.

When Mary was a toddler, Jacob would take her with him when he went to the olive grove to take care of the trees. She would ride atop her father's shoulders and stay with him until the mid-day meal. She felt like a big girl and knew in some way that she was helping.

This time was Naomi's to do the household chores at her leisure without interruptions from the child. Naomi still had to be careful not to overexert herself. She never was very strong after the ordeal of Mary's birth.

Her mother was getting older now so much was expected of the girl. Mary Saphronia was married with children of her own and Thomas was now a man.

❧∽❧

How is your father doing? He is feeling better, I hope", Mary Elizabeth said with full sincerity.

"He is doing much better. He is still not ready to be up and about, but I do not think it will be much longer. Mother asked the

7

Rabbi to look in on him a couple of times today while we were gone and he had done fine.

"You did not come over here just to ask about my father. It is fully dark now. What is so important that it could not wait until tomorrow?"

Mary breathed a big sigh of frustration. Mary Elizabeth *was* her best friend but would she please get to the point.

"Mary, I found out late last night that I am to be betrothed to John", Mary Elizabeth chortled.

"John who?" asked Mary teasing. In all reality, she knew who he was.

"Benjamin Levi's son, you know, John, the baker's son. He is so handsome. I never imagined that he would want to marry me", she said as she held her skirt out and twirled around in a kind of girlish dance.

"I *have* seen him watching me as I have passed by, but who would have thought that he would want to marry me!?" I know, I have seen him looking at you, too", Mary said with a giggle.

Mary Elizabeth looked surprised and then commented, "And you did not tell me? I cannot believe that you did not say something. We are so close; I thought you told me everything."

"Well, sometimes it is more fun to keep some things to oneself."

Then getting back to the subject at hand Mary Elizabeth continued, "The betrothal will be announced tomorrow in the Synagogue after worship.

"I was hoping it would be he who would ask for my hand, but I really did not expect it. There are so many other eligible girls in the village." She seemed to be rattling on.

Mary gave her friend a big hug, hoping that would be the end of the conversation so she could get back to her chores.

"Last night his father and mine were together at the Inn talking for two whole hours discussing the betrothal", Mary Elizabeth stated.

"When John's father came over I had no idea what it was about. I thought maybe he wanted to buy some sheep from my father.

"Who do you think you will be betrothed to, Mary?" the girl asked.

"I have no idea. I really have not given it much thought. I still feel like I am too young. Besides, I have not seen anyone *watching* me."

"I have", said Mary Elizabeth. "And besides, you are the same age as I", she said indignantly.

"Who, who, who has been watching me?"

"Oh Mary, I cannot believe that you have not noticed; the carpenter's son Joseph."

"I do not believe you, Mary Elizabeth", the friend said angrily. "Stop tormenting me. I have never seen him 'look at me', not even once. Why would he? He is so tall and so wonderful and so strong." Mary hung her head and then whispered, "and yet so gentle." Mary sighed deeply and then continued, "Although, I am getting *close* to marrying age, as far as I know, no one has asked for my hand", she said blatantly.

"Well, I still think it will be Joseph", Mary Elizabeth said as she gave Mary a quick hug and bounced off toward her house.

Mary Elizabeth suddenly turned and looked at Mary, "It would be wonderful if we could both be married at the same time", she said as an afterthought. "Remember, we *are* just like sisters, maybe even closer than some real sisters. You will tell me right away if he asks for your hand, right?

"You know I will." Then Mary sat on a large rock that was in front of her house and watched as her best friend skipped away. She sat there for some time thinking of the conversation they had just had and watching until Mary Elizabeth was out of sight.

Mary was very happy for her friend, but at the same time perplexed. Yes, she would like to get married...someday. She thought Joseph was wonderful, but why would he ever want to marry her. She had spoken to him a few times when she was younger, however, not enough for them to get to know each other. He was quite a bit older than she was. She was surprised that he had not already married someone else. She had seen him many times while she was growing up; nevertheless, she was sure he would not be the one who would ask for her hand. Mary Elizabeth must be wrong.

As Mary entered her house, her mother could tell something was bothering her. She looked so distant, as though she was in some strange far off land. Not at all like her daughter.

"Mary, what is wrong. Is something wrong with Mary Elizabeth or her family?"

"No, Mama", the daughter said unconvincingly. She tried to cheer up as she continued, "Mary Elizabeth and John bar Benjamin are to be betrothed."

"Wonderful, but why are you so sullen? This is good."

"Yes, Mama, I know it is and I am very happy for them."

"You do not look very happy, Daughter. Are you afraid you are going to lose your best friend?"

"No, I know we will always be friends. We have always been like sisters. She just said something disturbing that I do not fully understand", Mary said slowly. "Mary Elizabeth said that Joseph, you know the carpenter's son, has been watching me. I have not seen him. She seems to think that he will be asking for my hand."

"Well, what do you think about that?" Naomi asked.

"I am not sure. I know that Joseph is a wonderful man. He makes a good living. He is highly respected as a carpenter and as a man. When his father retires he will take over the business with some of his younger brothers. I am sure he will make someone a good husband. I am really surprised he has not married already. But why would he want to marry me? I just do not know what to think", the girl said thoughtfully.

"Do you think you would want to marry Joseph?" her mother surveyed as she washed the vegetables from her garden.

"I had not really thought at all about marriage until a few minutes ago", Mary answered, and then started cutting the cheese into bite-size pieces.

"I have not been ready for marriage, so therefore, I had not given any thought to who my future husband might be. Mary Elizabeth and I use to play with our dolls and pretend we were married, but that was a long time ago."

"No thoughts went through your mind that Joseph might be interested in you as a possible wife?" her mother queried.

"No, have you heard anything?"

"People in the village have teased for years that the reason Joseph has not married is because he was waiting for you to grow up and be of marrying age. You never heard anything like that?" Naomi asked as she put the vegetables on a platter and reached for the bread.

"I had heard it when I was a child, but I never paid attention to it. You know how people like to gossip", Mary returned as she was putting the cheese board on the table.

"Yes, but maybe there was some truth to that statement. He could have married any number of girls in this village and probably even more in the surrounding villages. And why has he not? Maybe he really *has* been waiting for you.

"Go call your father and brother for supper", Naomi said as she smiled at her daughter.

"Papa is well enough to eat with us?"

"He is feeling much better and is tired of lying around. He feels like he must do something."

Mary felt relieved that her father was well enough to join them for supper and also because that ended the conversation about Joseph.

She was still sure that he would not be the one she would marry.

೩•೮

Mary Elizabeth was very deep in thought as she approached the door that led into her home; the home that her father had built just after Theresa and he had married and moved to Nazareth.

Until the house was finished they had lived in a tent on the property. Theresa did not mind living in the tent. She knew it would not be very long before she would have a home of her own. Her family would have been mortified if they had known she was living in a tent. How degrading that would have been. So that was her secret. She would never tell. The beautiful young woman would have been willing to live anywhere as long as she and Abraham could be together.

The house was very comfortable; maybe not like her sisters were used to, but none-the-less, one of the better homes in Nazareth. Mary Elizabeth was proud of the home which she shared with her with her parents, Abraham and Theresa, her brother, Abraham, named for his father, called Abby, and her sister, Sarah; both younger than she.

She headed straight to the room where she slept and lay on her straw bed not noticing that her mother was fixing the evening meal with the help of Sarah. She was too preoccupied, thinking about her conversation with Mary.

☙◦❧

[Mary is much more beautiful than I am and I cannot understand why Joseph has not asked for her hand. It is obvious to everyone in the village, except Mary, that he loves her and longs to be with her. There are other unmarried girls in the village, too. Why he has not been interested in one of them is a mystery to me.

Maybe Joseph is taking his time with his decision. He *does* seem to be very conscientious. And besides, that is not a decision that should be made lightly, after all, divorce, should never be an option. I know it happens, but not to anyone I know. I doubt if there has ever been a divorce in Nazareth.

Maybe Mary will not be his choice after all. There are many other maidens in this village, even Sarah, although, she is still too young. But she will not be in a couple of years. Let me think; there is Rebekah, Rachel, Anna, Mary Isabel, Esther, Judith and Hannah, but then Hannah is his sister... No, it has to be Mary. I *have* seen him watching her several times. I cannot believe that Mary has not noticed. I think he has been very obvious. I am sure other people have been aware of his stares.

Usually unmarried men do not noticeably look at a maiden unless they are interested. They may look, but not stare. I have not seen him look at any of the others. Of course, I am usually with Mary so I probably would not have noticed. Yes, it has to be her.

Joseph is not getting any younger. He is a couple of years older than John. He must make his mind up soon as to whom he will marry or there will not be a maiden around that would want him because he will be too old and wrinkly.]

She had to smile to herself with the thought of Joseph with white hair and a long beard still working in his father's carpenter shop.

"Mary Elizabeth, will you milk the goat so we can have supper, you know how your father loves his goat's milk", her mother called from the cooking area.

Her train of thought was interrupted, "Yes, Mama", she returned half-heartedly.

[Yes, he does love his goat's milk, but I hate milking the goat. She smells awful. Besides, she always looks at me contrarily. I am afraid one of these days she will bite me again. The last time she bit me, it bled for a long time. Mama wrapped it for me, but it left a bad scar on my hand. Why do I have to milk the goat? Sarah could do it. I would much rather help Mama with the food. I do not mind helping with the cooking.]

Mary Elizabeth knew she had spent far too much time talking to Mary when she should have been home helping her mother, but she just could not wait. Mary would want to know right away. She could not keep this good news from her very long and she would not want to. Besides, maybe this was her mother's way of letting her know that next time she had better pay more attention to her duties instead of thinking about her fantasies and spending so much time with Mary.

[I do not *always* have fantasies. I have thoughts about reality, too. But my fantasies are a lot more fun], she mused as she flipped her long dark hair with a jerk.

Mary Elizabeth put her shawl over her head, lit a lantern, got the stool and pail and exited out the back way.

[I had better hurry. I am going to have a hard time finding the goat, not alone getting her to stand still while she is being milked] She spied her eating some grass behind some bushes. "Come here, Helena."

She had named the goat after one of her aunts who she did not particularly care for and she did not care much for goats either.

❧◦❧

Aunt Helena was a fat woman with a high pitched, squeaky voice, which pierced to the very core of one's brain each time she spoke. She was as loud as the horn that called the Elders to Assembly. She loved calling Abraham names like "worthless, lazy, and good-for-nothing except herding sheep".

Abraham did not let it bother him. He was quite passive when it came to Theresa's family. He could not see any sense in upsetting his wife. But the names had always irritated Mary Elizabeth because she loved her father very much. Besides, he earned a very fine living for his family.

Aunt Helena was her mother's sister, who lived in Jerusalem, and had always felt that Theresa had married far below what had been expected of her.

Her father had been a lawyer in Jerusalem and was highly respected in his field. It had been assumed that Theresa would marry someone of high status and live in Jerusalem as the other daughters had. But she had fallen in love with a young shepherd boy named Abraham.

↾•↽

One day, long ago, as Theresa was walking on the highway outside of Jerusalem, she had spied him sitting on the ground under a Eucalyptus tree, chewing on a long blade of grass.

[Who is this man who watches me so intently? I come here every day to see him. He watches every move I make. I wish he would speak to me. I could speak to him first, but that would not be proper. I will walk slowly to give him the chance to say something...if he wants to. He was so tall and lean and had such sad, little boy eyes she could not help falling in love with him. Besides, he looked so wonderfully cute in his shepherd garb with his long staff that she could not resist his charm.]

She watched him shyly out of the corner of her eye. Theresa knew he was watching, but he said and did nothing. She just kept on walking.

He definitely was interested in Theresa, but he too, was shy and did not know what to say.

[Who is this beautiful creature that walks by every day? She must be of royalty. She dresses so fine. Should I speak to her? No! I do not dare. I would never be good enough for her. I am just a poor shepherd boy. No, I must say nothing to her. But her eyes seem to be beckoning me. I must be imagining it. She would never want to talk to a mere shepherd.]

Abraham looked down at the grass. He plucked another long blade and placed it strategically between his two front teeth. He then looked at the girl. Slowly, he managed to get to his feet. He felt weak and sick to his stomach. His knees felt as if they would not support his body. He surely did not want to trip and fall in front of this lovely woman. He did not want to appear clumsy. He stood for a moment to steady himself against the tree. When he felt as if he had control, he walked to the side of the road.

Theresa was just approaching near where he was standing. He was even more handsome up close than she had thought before. She had been walking this way for about two weeks and this was the first time he had come to the edge of the road. He *must* want to say *something*.

What would he say? He did not want to sound foolish. He did not want to stutter or stammer. He wanted to sound *somewhat* intelligent.

"Shalom." [Now that did not hurt.]

"Shalom", Theresa returned shyly. Then she walked on.

"What is your name?" Abraham said, trying to start a conversation.

"Theresa, what is yours?" She stopped and looked into his eyes.

He had wonderful eyes, so rich and brown.

Well, this was a beginning. Now what?

"My name is Abraham. I tend sheep for my father. There he is standing on the hill over there", he said pointing in the direction of a tall man.

[Now, what do *I* say? It is my turn to keep this conversation going.]

"I like your coat", Theresa stated as she looked at him without raising her head.

[Did I sound silly? I really do like it.]

"Thank you, my mother made it for me. She thought this is what 'Joseph's Coat of Many Colors' must have looked like. I like it, too."

Theresa whispered shyly, "I must be going. Mother will wonder where I have gone, although she knows I love to walk." "Will you be back tomorrow?" Abraham questioned.

"Maybe", that was the only answer that would come out of her mouth. She turned and hurried back toward the city.

[Of course she would be back. Now that he had finally spoken to her, she knew she could not stay away.]

After that day Theresa seemed to spend a lot of time talking to the shepherd boy on long afternoons. Her mother had gotten suspicious and had questioned the girl about her absences, so she was not entirely surprised when her daughter told her of her feelings for the shepherd boy.

Abraham and Theresa saw each other just about every day, except on the Sabbath. Theresa's mother was the only one who knew anything about the secret romance. This went on for several months.

One evening Abraham made the mistake of going to Theresa's father to ask for her hand in marriage instead of having his father ask for him.

When the boy told him he could not pay for the privilege of marrying his daughter, the elder Benjamin Eliesar just laughed and sent him away dejected.

That night at the supper table the story had been related to the rest of the family. Theresa's father had thrown back his head and roared with a belly laugh that only he could do. In fact, he laughed so hard that he nearly went over backwards in his chair. Theresa had run to her bed crying. It so surprised her father that all he could do was stare into space, wondering what he had said what was wrong. Surely she could not possibly be interested in marrying a common shepherd. That would be disgraceful.

Theresa's mother, Leah, had shushed him and followed her daughter to her room where she discovered Theresa's true feelings for Abraham, the shepherd boy. With that, the betrothal had been finalized and after a suitable amount of time, Abraham and Theresa were married. They settled in Nazareth with the responsibility of a few sheep, which were given to him as a wedding present by his father.

҉҉

Mary Elizabeth had always loved that story and had had her parents repeat it often when she was younger, although, with the ensuing years, it had blossomed and become much spicier.

Abraham had hired some boys to help herd his sheep. That was the sad thing about having only one son; he did not have enough help. He loved Abby but was saddened at not having had a dozen sons.

He had gone to some of the nearby villages to inquire if there were any young men who would be interested in herding sheep. He had found five and brought them home with him.

They watched over the sheep at night to keep the wolves and thieves away while Abraham and Abby watched them during the day.

He treated the boys like his own sons. They slept in the shed during the day and ate at Abraham's table. When he paid them, they would take the money back to their respective villages and give it to their parents. They had no need for money. They had everything they could want or need at Abraham's house.

҉҉

"Come here, you worthless animal. How can I milk you over there? You should know it is getting late."

It was obvious the goat was unaware of time. She did not budge, and was content to keep eating the lush greens. So the girl took her utensils and the lantern and went to the goat. It was evident that she was ready to be milked.

[Her milk sack looks as if it is ready to burst. She should have come and saved me the anguish of having to carry everything to her; although, it is apparent that she does not care.]

17

She carefully sat down on the three-legged stool. She did not want to fall or upset Helena or she might have to catch her somewhere else. Once was enough.

As she was milking, Mary Elizabeth could hear her father outside in front of the house talking to some of the Elders.

"Yes, my Mary Elizabeth will marry John. He is a good man and will make her a fine husband. His father came to me last night and *begged* for my daughter's hand for his son over some cheese and a cask of fine wine at Simon's Inn", Abraham boasted as all proud fathers must.

Then someone teased, "Yes, with all of the baked goods he makes, what he does not sell will make your Mary Elizabeth as fat as one of your old ewes".

"Ah, but she will be a happy old ewe", her father retorted. And all the men laughed loudly. Abraham had a wonderful sense of humor and he was not about to let anyone else have the last laugh.

Mary Elizabeth sighed. She did not want to be fat like Aunt Helena. She could just imagine herself waddling around trying hard to keep the house clean while chewing on a large piece of bread laden with butter and honey, while making John put her sandals on for her because she could not reach her feet. No, that just would not do at all.

She took an even deeper breath this time. She knew that her father was teasing, but the words still stung.

She did not pay attention to anything else the men were saying, but she could still hear the laughter. All that she could think about was getting the goat milked before the rest of the meal was ready.

☙❧

At the dinner table Abraham asked Mary Elizabeth, "Did Mary say anything to you today about her betrothal to Joseph?"

She looked at him startled and then answered, "No, Papa, she and her mother were gone to the market in Sappora most of the day. She did not get home until just before supper. Why, have you heard something?"

"Well, maybe it has not happened yet", Abraham said almost in a whisper as he leaned forward on one elbow and cupped his hand next to his mouth, pretending that it might be a well-kept secret, but making sure everyone at the table heard.

Then as he continued to eat, he added, with his mouth full of the wonderful mutton Theresa had served, "Some of the Elders and I were discussing it a little while ago. It is just a matter of time, you know", as he wiped his mouth with the sleeve of his shirt.

Mary Elizabeth knew he was right but was surprised to hear her father say so. She had thought she was the only one that was privy to that kind of information. After all, they *were* like sisters. Mary would have told her first, especially after the conversation they had just had. No, it had not happened yet. But she too knew that it would.

Abraham continued again, not noticing Mary Elizabeth's reaction, "We were all thinking that Joseph better hurry and ask for her hand. If he waits too long someone else will." He gulped another mouthful of the succulent meat, "I will wager one of my best sheep that Joseph's father will pay quite a handsome price for her hand".

He was still whispering, which was starting to irritate Mary Elizabeth. Abby was holding his mouth and giggling softly so he would not upset his father. Not that he would notice anyway. He was too busy contemplating Mary's worth.

Then Theresa said, mocking her husband's whisper leaning forward with her own hand cupped next to her mouth, "She *is* quite a prize".

[*Quite a prize!* That sounds as if he were buying a large milking cow. I wonder if John's father thought I was '*quite a prize*'. Actually, I was wondering what John's father did pay for my hand. I do not dare ask because I am just a woman and any business deals created would not be made known to me.

Sometimes I wish the daughter were in on the negotiations, if there were any. Maybe Papa did not ask much for me. That is silly! My father is a shrewd businessman. He would ask a high price for anything he sold. Oh, now I sound like I am a goat, an ass, or some other dumb animal. I am *not* for sale! At least my father will send me with a handsome dowry.]

Mary Elizabeth sat quietly during the rest of the meal as she considered what her worth might be.

When supper was finished, she and Sarah cleared the table and then Mary Elizabeth went to the well to draw water for drinking and to wash the dishes. She did not worry about it being dark. In all actuality, she rather enjoyed walking at night, although she did not do it much. It seemed much easier to think. There were not as many people around to interrupt the thinking process. However, if there were a caravan in the village, she would not go out alone at night at all.

She walked slowly to the well in the middle of the village hoping Mary would see her and want to talk some more. But she was nowhere to be found. She was probably eating her own meal.

She looked around warily feeling a presence, but she saw nothing. As she pulled the bucket up, she was startled when she felt a light tap on her shoulder.

It was Mary, "Are you done with supper?"

"I think Mama was upset with me because I was talking to you so long. She made me milk Helena. Was your mother angry?"

"No, she is used to our being together so much. She knew I would not be too long."

"I have had a hard time concentrating. I have so much on my mind", Mary Elizabeth stated.

Then her demeanor changed. She said with a new burst of energy, "My Papa asked about you tonight". She had a touch of sarcasm in her voice.

"Oh? And just what did he say?" Mary could not think of any reason her friend's father would ask about her except to be polite and ask of her welfare.

"He just asked if Joseph's father had asked for your hand for his son. That is all", Mary Elizabeth chortled.

"I wish people would quit worrying about me. I will probably end up being an old maid anyway", Mary said wistfully.

Mary Elizabeth laughed and said, "Oh Mary, you are so funny", and then added, "Papa says it is just a matter of time and I agree."

"Why would he say that? Has he heard something?"

"I do not know", Mary Elizabeth returned, now more serious. "He said he and the other Elders were talking about it before supper. That is all I know. Be patient and do not worry so much."

"I cannot help it; my best friend is betrothed and hears rumors about me. That is about all I will be able to think about. I will see you tomorrow."

Mary turned and walked away. She seemed to be in deep thought that no one could penetrate.

⊰•⊱

Women were subject to their husbands. 1 Peter 3:5 For after this manner in the old time the holy women also, who trusted in God, adorned themselves, being in subjection unto their own husbands Timothy 2:11 Let the woman learn in silence with all subjection. Ephesians 5:22 (Colossians 3:18), Wives, submit yourselves unto your own husbands, as unto the Lord.
Mary's sister Mary is found in John 19:25.

The information on the birth of children and the duties of midwives is found in "Celebrating Life: Jewish Rites of Passage", pp 6-7 by Malka Drucker.
The custom of the groom's father, in those days (biblical times) was to pay a mohar, or a bride's price, to the bride's father. This generally consisted of fifty shekels of silver was found in "Under the Wedding Canopy: Love and Marriage in Judaism" by David C. and Esther R. Gross, p. 193

CHAPTER
TWO

Joseph was busy at the workbench when John appeared at the door. "Do you have a minute?" John inquired.

"Come in. We can talk while I work."

Joseph and John had been close friends since they were children in school together. They both had excelled in the Talmud *and* the Torah. They had each said they wanted to be Rabbis when they grew up. Of course, that was when they were children. Things changed. Their fathers needed them in their businesses and they were content, for the most part.

❧❧

John came close to the workbench and inspected the item that Joseph was sanding with the sanding stone he held in his right hand. The item was a pestle he was making for the village doctor. The mortise was sitting on the workbench already finished.

"You do wonderful work. I wish I could make trees into beautiful works of art as you do", John remarked.

"Ah, my friend, you are an artist yourself. I could never make the delicious breads that you do."

❧❧

Complimenting each person you come in contact with was a way of life for men in this little village as well as others. It was the best way to show appreciation. If the first thing said was not a compliment, the person was thought to be an enemy. Even strangers

22

always found ways to complement their hosts. People were always careful not to give the wrong impression.

❧❦

"I would have thought the doctor would have wanted it made of stone."

"I agree, but I only do what I am asked to do. Maybe he wants to put it in the front window just to show people that he is the doctor. You know, just as an example, not the real thing."

"Maybe, I would never have thought of that."

"That is the only idea I can come up with."

John examined the workshop as he had done so many times in the past. On the wall hung the tools such as a number of saws, planes, mallets, hammers, chisels and others. They were all neatly hung so they would be within easy access when needed. On the floor next to the bench were small barrels of nails of different sizes and the small items used in the art of carpentry.

There was a small amount of sawdust on the floor where Joseph stood that had not been cleaned up as yet, however, John knew that it soon would be.

The place was always as neat as a pin. The father and son were fastidious about cleanliness. It would not do for customers to enter and find the shop in disarray. They might decide to take their business elsewhere. Although, this was the only carpenter shop in Nazareth. The other villages around each had at least one. However, it would not be wise to offend a valued patron.

❧❦

John continued, "I suppose you have heard that Mary Elizabeth and I are betrothed." You could see the pride and excitement in his eyes. Yes, the love was there, there was no mistaking that.

Joseph grinned at his friend and replied, "I had heard something to that effect. And, I must say, it is about time. I know how long it took you to get up the courage."

"Wait a minute. I would not talk if I were you. What about Mary? You said some time ago that you were going to get *your* father to ask for *her* hand", John touted in a voice loud enough that Joseph's father, Heli, who was in the back corner of the shop could hear also.

They loved to tease one another. They had been like brothers ever since they had met.

⮞⮜

John's father Benjamin and his wife, Mary Anna came to Nazareth when John was just five years old.

"What is this?" Heli asked as he came forward so he could hear well. "You love a girl and I am the last to know? What kind of son are you?" Heli teased, "Does your mother know?"

"No, Father. I have not said anything to anyone except John, and that was as an afterthought and clearly a mistake. I did not realize he was going to make a public issue of it", Joseph stated as he glared at his friend.

He was not really angry with Joseph. The whole conversation was done in a fun and joking manner.

"You wish to have her hand? Why did you not tell me? I was beginning to think you would never marry. Tell me, which Mary is it?" Heli could jest with the best of them. He had always been such a tease that his wife did not know when he was serious and when he was not.

"Oh, Father, now which Mary could it be?"

Heli knew, of course, but it was always fun to act confused over such matters until it was confirmed.

"She is a beautiful woman and will make someone a fine wife if…he does not wait *too* long. You know, some young man who is not afraid to speak up may ask for her hand if someone else is too slow."

To put in a dig now and then by his father seemed to keep Joseph on his toes.

"Father, when I feel the time is right I will let you know. In fact, you will be the first to know. And if Jehovah thinks she is the wife for me, no one else will ask, or her father will refuse. I want to be sure *I* am ready."

"Joseph, Joseph, Joseph, I wonder if you will ever be ready", Heli said with a sly little grin on his bearded face.

❧❧

Heli was a small man, unlike his son who derived his height from his mother's side of the family. He was rotund, but firm. He did enjoy his wife's cooking; maybe a little more than was necessary, but then, his wife was known for her wonderful meals. John always felt privileged to be asked to stay for dinner at Joseph's home.

Heli was firm because of his hard work at being a carpenter. His hair was graying quickly these days, but black was still dominant. His eyes had a certain twinkle in them, which made one know he was more than just a little impish. He was a Jew by birth, being of the House of David, through the line of Jesse. But as other Jews he knew, he preferred the hills and quiet seclusion of the Galilean countryside to the region around Bethlehem. However, being very devout, he spent as much time in the Synagogue as possible. With Joseph able to work the shop by himself, Heli was able to spend a lot less time there, although, he still enjoyed being there now and again. He was definitely a craftsman and he had taught Joseph well. He was proud of his eldest son, as any father would be.

He had been quite ill of late, but he was starting to feel much better. He was beginning to spend a little more time in the shop, however, not as much as he would like. He still tired quickly. He also felt that he had been neglecting his worship time.

Many of the villagers had succumbed to this sickness including his brother Jacob. It seemed to strike at least one member of every family. Very few families escaped the malady.

❧❧

Joseph continued the conversation, "When did it take place, John?"

"What?" was the question.

"You know, the talk between Abraham and your father.

25

"I spoke to my father a short time ago and it was agreed by both he and the Rabbi, that Mary Elizabeth would be a suitable wife for me. He went to her house last evening and asked if he could talk to Abraham at the Inn.

"The rest was fairly simple, you know, the wine, the talk, and the joviality, the hugs and kisses on the cheeks, the discussion of the betrothal, the gifts and the dowry. And then more wine, of course. It took quite a long time. I guess Abraham is quite the negotiator.

"I like Abraham. He is a good man", Heli interjected.

"Yes, Father, so do I", said Joseph, wondering where this conversation was leading.

"I just hope all will go as smoothly when I speak to Jacob", his father hinted to Joseph. "And so, how long have you loved Mary?"

"When I was younger, I watched Mary as she would go to the well for water. I thought she was beautiful then, but I have seen her bloom into the delightful flower she is today. I have known for a couple of years now that I wanted her to be my wife someday.

Joseph was caught up in his thoughts of Mary. He mused at the thought of her one day being his own betrothed, and then his wife.

But he was not ready for such a thing yet.

"If someone else does not ask for her hand first", Heli retorted.

Joseph was startled out of his revelry and then replied, "Father I have a lot to do before I can even foresee any time when it might be possible to seek her hand.

John feeling left out of the conversation, decided to jump in, "Hah, what do you have to do? I cannot even imagine anything that could be more important than being with the one you love."

"Well…before I get married, I want to have a suitable home to give to Mary with some nice furniture. I want to be sure she will be comfortable. I cannot even hope that she would be willing to marry a pauper."

"You are not a pauper", Heli returned, feeling a little hurt. "I give you good wages. That should be sufficient."

"Forgive me, Father. I did not mean it that way. I live very comfortably. It is just that I want everything to be perfect for my wife. I want to give her everything she needs and desires."

"Joseph, Joseph, Joseph you will have plenty of time after you are betrothed", Heli said sorrowfully. "You will probably not marry for a year or more".

"That is true, but I want to be sure I am ready for something of that importance."

"Always the practical one, he has already made a bed and some chairs and a very sturdy table, and that was before I even knew that he had someone in mind to marry", Heli stated as he looked at John, hoping for some support for his cause.

Joseph ignored the look and asked, "When will the Betrothal Feast be, John?"

"That is what I came to talk to you about. Could I hire you to make a small box for me? I want to give it to Mary Elizabeth at the feast on Thursday evening. The Betrothal Feast will be announced at the Sabbath Service tomorrow. Will that give you enough time? I wanted *you* to make it because I know that you are the best carpenter around.

"Joseph, when are you going to ask for Mary's hand? Soon?" his friend inquired.

"Maybe", Joseph said quickly and then added before anyone could question him more about that subject, "John would you like to stay for supper?"

"Thank you, but not tonight. There is much to be done and Mother is expecting me."

Joseph looked at his father and said, "You should go home and have supper. Please tell Mother that I will be along soon, but not to wait for me. I need to clean up here first".

Heli knew that Joseph wanted to be alone with John, so feeling dispirited and being very tired, he retreated out the door, but turned to say, "Try not to be too long. You know how your mother worries." With that he was gone.

"Thank you so much for bringing up Mary around my father", Joseph said sarcastically.

"I am sorry, I thought he knew", John said apologetically. Then as an afterthought he added, "Everyone else in the village knows. I imagine even Mary does. People have been talking about it for years.

You know how people talk, especially old men who have nothing better to do. Besides, you are taking much too long. You should have been betrothed by now. Waiting can be dangerous, you know."

"I doubt I have much to worry about. I have not seen many eligible young men hanging around, beating down her door to ask for her hand. And I am almost ready. I have accomplished a lot lately. I have decided that I will build our house by Mary's favorite place, you know, the rock where Mary and Mary Elizabeth go to talk. I think that would be the perfect place for our home."

That took John totally by surprise and then he replied, "When are you going to start the house?"

"Right after my father asks for her hand. That will be my surprise and one of my gifts to her. I think it will please her. She seems to be the sentimental type. I have kept a close eye on her in the last few years without trying to let her know."

"I never knew you were such a romantic, Joseph".

"I have my moments", Joseph said as he smiled sheepishly.

"You have no idea if she knows of your feelings for her?"

"I really do not think so. I have tried to be very discreet", Joseph whispered.

"What if she does not want her house built there? Then what are you going to do?. She and Mary Elizabeth will not have their retreat anymore", John said concerned.

"I really do not know. I will think about that when the time comes. Right now, I think it is a wonderful idea. I hope she will think so, too. Hopefully, by then she and Mary Elizabeth will not feel as if they need a retreat."

John picked up the broom and started sweeping the floor where Heli had been working. "Women always need a place where they can go to be alone to talk about woman stuff. It is just their nature. Just like you and I meet here to talk about man stuff."

Joseph said nothing more and started putting the tools away. He did have a lot to think about, though. Things he had been thinking about for some time, but had not had the nerve to say out loud. Maybe it *was* time to say what was on his mind. Maybe he had had the same thoughts at one time. He could tell John.

"John, I am afraid to ask for Mary's hand", Joseph stated in almost a whisper, not looking his friend in the eye.

John raised his hand as if he was going to speak, but Joseph jumped in before his friend could say anything. Now, looking right into John's eyes he continued, "Hear me out, what if she does not want to marry me? What if she thinks I am not good enough for her? She is so beautiful and so amazing", he said thoughtfully. "What if she wants someone who is more suited for her and can take better care of her? I am just...a humble carpenter. What if I repulse her when she looks at me? What if she already has someone else in mind to marry?"

"Hold on a minute. Stop with the 'what ifs'", said his friend trying to get a word in edgewise. "You are being foolish. There is no one better for her than you because I am already taken", John said jokingly with a grin on his face as big as all outdoors.

Joseph looked at John and laughed good-heartedly and slapped him on the back.

"You do not understand. I am serious. What if she *really does not* want to marry me?"

"Of course she would. You have everything to offer her", he said as he swept his hand outward in front of him as a gesture.

"You make a fine living. Your father will soon be retiring and you will be taking over this great establishment. You are a very able craftsman. Men from far and wide envy your handiwork.

"Think, man, any woman would feel lucky to have you for a husband. You are kind, gentle: maybe a little sappy at times. You are fairly nice looking, not as good looking as I, but you will do."

John was trying very hard to bring up his spirits, but he was not having much success.

Joseph just grinned and continued the conversation, "Humility never was one of your finer qualities. I understand what you are trying to do, but I am just not convinced."

"Good grief, man, what does it take to convince you that you had better move on this matter. You are not getting any younger. If you are ever going to get married and have children you had better get started.

"Mary is a great woman, almost as good as Mary Elizabeth", John snickered, "But we will not get into that. She has had good upbringing. She *is* beautiful. She is from the same lineage as you. She is young and strong. I cannot figure what else you could want."

"What did you do, check her teeth, too? You sound as if I am intending to buy a fine steed."

Joseph took the broom from John and put it into its little niche where it belonged. He sat on the stool by the workbench and put his elbows on his knees with his head down, supported by both hands at his temples. It was evident the agony he was going through.

"I do not know what I want or what I expect. I am aware of all of Mary's significant qualities", Joseph said almost in a whisper.

John hesitated and then said, "Maybe your father and I are putting too much pressure on you." He patted his friend softly on the back and continued, "I will leave you alone to think by yourself. I am going home now. If you decide you want someone to talk to, I will be there. What about the box?"

"I will make you a fine box and have it ready by Thursday.

Thank you for listening to my problems. Your friendship means a lot to me. I am just confused. I have to do things my own way and in my own time", Joseph said.

The oil in the lamps had gone almost completely out when the door shut. Joseph was alone with his thoughts. As the lights flickered, they gave off an eerie sensation. Somehow, he felt he was not entirely alone.

He looked around the room. No one was there. Why was he feeling this way? What was going on?

He put his head back down in the same position as before. A silent prayer for guidance was said:

[Lord, I try not to bother you too much. I know you have more important things to do besides listening to me. I know how busy you must be. I also know that I am very insignificant and that others need your help much more than I do, but please help me just this once.

I am so confused. I do not know what is right or what is wrong.

30

I know all of Mary's attributes. I can find no fault with her. How am I to know what is right? Should I ask for Mary's hand? Should I look for another? Should I remain celibate?

I want to marry. I do not want to be alone in my later years when my family is all gone. I want children. I want sons that I can train to be carpenters as my father taught me and my brothers. I want to be as happy as my parents are.

Please, Jehovah, help me to understand my feelings and guide me in the right direction. Amen.]

He continued to sit silently in that same position for a long time. All of a sudden everything became very clear. He knew what he must do.

☙◦❧

John decided that instead of going straight home he would take a walk.

He started toward the edge of town. He really did not have any specific place in mind. He had a lot of questions on his mind. Marriage was a serious subject and he was having serious doubts. Not about his love for Mary Elizabeth, he had doubts about himself.

[Am I ready for this? Am I stable enough to get married? Will I be a good husband and father?

I do not know. Maybe Joseph had the right idea. Maybe I should be more prepared. Maybe I should have had more things put away before I made this big decision.]

Before he knew it, he was at Mary Elizabeth's and Mary's favorite spot, the same rock where unknowingly Mary Elizabeth had been just hours earlier.

[I can see why this place is so special. The view from here is spectacular. The moon is so big and bright. The stars look as though I could reach up and pluck one from the sky. If only I could, I would grab a whole armful of them and take them to Mary Elizabeth to show her how much I cherish her. She is perfect for me. I love everything about her. I have adored her for at least two years. I have watched her emerge from her cocoon to a lovely, elusive butterfly.

31

This woman has a wildness about her that makes her more alluring than anyone I have ever known. She is as a lioness waiting to be tamed; a wild flower waiting to be nurtured.

Is she ready for marriage? Is she having any second thoughts about me? Does she love me? Will I have to wait until after our marriage for her to blossom?

Will she come to my bed willingly or will I have to wait and be gentle and patient with her. I would never want to break her spirit.

I have this ache deep down inside me. An ache that will not be appeased until Mary Elizabeth is totally mine.]

John climbed up on the rock and sat down and just looked in every direction. He felt so inconsequential; so small. The world around him seemed so immense. What lies out there beyond those green, lush hills now turned black with the night?

Yes, Jerusalem. He had been there many times. Jerusalem was a special place where he had gone with his father for certain Holy Days. In a few years he would be able to take his own son, if Jehovah wills.

What lies beyond Jerusalem? What great kingdoms are out there? Does it all have to belong to the Romans? Does the whole world belong to the Romans? When will the Messiah come to end the bondage? It cannot be too soon, that is for sure.

❧❦

"You are late for supper, My Son", Mary Anna said.

"Forgive me, Mother, I have had a lot on my mind", John explained. "I stopped to see Joseph. I wanted to be sure that he had heard about my betrothal to Mary Elizabeth and ask him if he would make a box for me to give to her at the ceremony.

"When I left the carpenter's shop I took a walk out to that big rock on the edge of the village. I sat, thought, and looked at the moon and stars.

"Is there any supper left?"

Mary Anna knew he was troubled because he was a good son and would not be disrespectful by not letting someone know where he was and he surely would not miss supper. She also knew that if he wanted to talk, he would probably go to his father. They were very close.

John went to the cupboard and took the supper that his mother had set aside for him. He broke off a big hunk of bread and took the meal and sat at the table. He ate slowly. He really was not in the mood to eat, but he felt that if he did not eat it would hurt his mother's feelings. She would think that he did not like her choice of supper she had cooked, although he ate every other night. In fact, he thought she was the best cook in the whole world.

After he finished his meal, he gave his mother a hard hug and retired to the roof to sit and talk with his father.

Benjamin Levi was startled as John walked up behind him. He had been watching the stars as he meditated about the events of the day.

John sat quietly for what seemed like a long time. He wanted to talk, but did not quite know how to begin. He did not want to sound immature, especially at his age. He was a man and wanted to sound like one.

Looking down as he was fidgeting with his hands he began, "Father, were you ever unsure as to whether you should marry Mother?"

Benjamin could tell that he was dead serious. "Son, do you have a problem?"

"I am having doubts. I love Mary Elizabeth, but I am not sure that I am ready for marriage. I am really confused. I had not realized it until I was talking to Joseph tonight.

Benjamin stared ahead for a couple of minutes in deep thought, which seemed like hours to John, "I think all men go through that. I know I did, but you must never tell your mother. She thinks that I have always been secure about our marriage. In actuality, I was scared to death. I was not sure I could make enough money to support us. I did not know if I would make a good husband and father. I knew I loved your mother with all of my heart, but I was not sure that was enough."

Benjamin looked back at the stars contemplating what his son was going through and what he might say next.

After a couple of minutes, John looked at his father and asked, "Do women go through the same things. Do they have the same feelings?"

"No, women are much stronger than men. They always seem to know their feelings. When they love someone they are ready for total commitment. They are not put together like men. Men only act like they have their feelings in perspective. In reality, men are cowards. Do not ever tell anyone that I said that, because I will deny the whole conversation", Benjamin teased.

"Father, I know it is not manly to say such a thing, but I want to say it now before I lose my nerve... I love you. You and Mother have always been so good to me. I have always been able to talk to you. I know you will always be there for me."

About that time Mary Anna joined them. She walked up to John and gave him a big hug. When he looked at her, she had a big tear glistening in one corner of her eye. Nothing more needed to be said.

John knew he must wrestle with his problem himself, but it was good to know that Mother and Father cared and would help him any way they could.

His mother sat down between her two men and they all looked at the stars and thought about the future.

కోుడ్

John could not sleep. He *was* tired, however, he had too much on his mind to think about sleeping. He decided that maybe if he walked for a while, he might be able to sort things out. He really wanted to see Mary Elizabeth, but knew that she would be sleeping. This was not any time for a visit anyway.

After a few minutes he found himself at the rock once again. He climbed up and sat down to think. What was the answer? Was he crazy to feel the doubt he was feeling? John knew he should not think this way.

He looked at the sky. A shooting star shot from the west to the east until it was out of sight. Staring at the horizon was not doing any good. It was still late at night. The sun would not be up for many hours.

He lay on the flat surface on his back and put his hands under his head and just looked around the heavens. Soon he fell asleep.

༺ༀ༒༻

In "Jesus The Christ" by James E. Talmage it states on p. 89, The writer of the article "Genealogy of Jesus Christ" in Smith's Bible Dict. Says: "The New Testament gives the genealogy of one person, our Savior (Matt. 1; Luke 3)... The following propositions will explain the true construction of these genealogies (so Lord A. C. Hervey): 1. It is both the genealogies of Joseph, i.e. of Jesus Christ, as the reputed and legal son of Joseph and Mary. 2. The genealogy of Matthew is Joseph's genealogy as legal successor to the throne of David.

That of Luke is Joseph's private genealogy, exhibiting his real birth, as David's son, and thus showing why he was heir to Solomon's crown. The simple principle that one evangelist exhibits that genealogy which contained the successive heirs to David's and Solomon's throne, while the other exhibits the paternal stem of him who was the heir, explains all the anomalies of the two pedigrees, their agreements as well as their discrepancies, and the circumstance of their being two at all. 3. Mary, the mother of Jesus, was probably the daughter of Jacob, and first cousin to Joseph her husband.

CHAPTER
THREE

Mary Elizabeth woke up just as the sun was rising. It was going to be a clear, sunny day. It would not dare to be any other way. She was feeling especially good. This day was going to be a happy one.

The bride-to-be lay on her bed stretching and smiling. This was the Sabbath. This was the day John would stand beside her as her groom.

Even though, they were not actually getting married right away, a betrothal was the next thing to it. They were going to belong to each other.

Soon Theresa was in the room with a pan of water and some clean cloths, "Mary Elizabeth... Sarah, it is time you two were up. There is a lot to do".

Sarah jumped up and exclaimed, "Mary Elizabeth, we have to get up! Today is the Sabbath. Your betrothal will be announced. You must be excited. I am excited and it is not even my betrothal. Come, get up".

Sarah was so nervous that when she reached for a cloth to wash up she dropped it on the floor. She bent over and picked it up. But when she came back up the girl bumped the edge of the pan of water which sent the water cascading to the floor in a large pool. Sarah plopped down on the floor next to the puddle, covered her face with the cloth and sobbed. "I am so sorry for making a mess. I will clean it up."

Mary Elizabeth just lay there stretching every muscle possible. She was oblivious to what was going on around her. She had more important things on her mind.

Sarah cleaned up the water and soon the whole family was up, washed, dressed and performing their Sabbath devotions.

಄

The Synagogue stood on the highest hill in Nazareth and faced Jerusalem as all Synagogues did. It was a tradition.

It was especially exhilarating today to watch the men in their long flowing Sabbath robes filing into the building. Mary Elizabeth had a feeling of awe as she watched the procession.

The women and children made their way to the Women's Gallery while the men were below. The building rang with the chants and psalms the men sang. Somewhere down there sat Abraham, Benjamin and John.

It was time for the reading of the Torah. The candlestick had been lighted and was shining brightly. The curtains to the dais were opened and the holy chest was unlocked. The Priest brought the sacred scrolls forward. Next the chosen seven would be called. Among the seven were Benjamin, Abraham and John because of the betrothal announcement.

When there was a betrothal, the groom's father would speak, next was the bride's father and lastly the groom himself. What an honor it was. Every groom looked forward to this day when he was called on to read from the Torah.

The "Seven" delivered the Hebrew passages, which were interpreted into Aramaic so that all could understand. Aramaic was the universal language.

When the last verse of the Torah was delivered by John, he lifted the Torah high over his head and the Rabbi arose. He motioned for John and Mary Elizabeth to come forward and stand beside each other. Then he said, "John bar Benjamin, known to here assembled, desires the hand of Mary Elizabeth, daughter of Abraham, whose lineage is of the House of David. If any here present have just cause to question this union, let him come forth now and make his protests known."

Everything was quiet. No one spoke a word. A cough could be heard somewhere in the back.

Then the Rabbi pronounced a blessing on the two lovers, "I bless John and Mary Elizabeth with prosperity, long life, love and many children. Amen".

At the end of the service all the men crowded around John to congratulate him with hugs and kisses on the cheeks. The same was happening with Mary Elizabeth in the Women's gallery.

෧๛๛

"Abby, you know Thursday is the day we are having the feast to celebrate John's and Mary Elizabeth's betrothal", his father announced. "You will go to the bakery to see if the breads will be ready. I ordered them Sunday. I just want to be sure. And take Mary Elizabeth with you. She can keep you company", he said teasingly.

His son was always called Abby by his father when Abraham was feeling especially jubilant, otherwise it was Abraham. Since John's father had spoken to Abraham he had been especially elated.

"But, Papa, I have not seen John since the Sabbath. I am concerned. What if he has had second thoughts about our marriage? Do I have to go? I would rather not go", the girl stated in her whiniest voice.

"Daughter, why would he have second thoughts about the marriage? If he were not pleased by you, he would not have had his father ask for your hand. Besides, you are going to have to see him sometime before the wedding.

"Be sure to ask about the rye bread", returned her mother as she glanced at her son.

"Yes Mama. Would you like to come with us, Sarah?" Abby asked.

"Oh, may I, Mama?"

"Of course", Theresa giggled.

Theresa is a large woman, however, not as large as Aunt Helena. She has large dark eyes that crinkle when she laughs. Mary Elizabeth hoped she could have her mother's compassion and love for her own children when they come along. Yes, her mother is the ideal woman. She would do well to be like her.

Mary Elizabeth stayed behind as Abby and Sarah started walking toward the bakery. Then, as soon as they were a short distance away, she ran close behind, hoping not to be seen. She wanted to sneak to the bakery without anyone noticing in case John was there. Mary Elizabeth was confused. She was not eager to see her betrothed. Well, actually she *did* want to see him. But she was afraid she would not know how to act around him. She had never had a hard time speaking with him before, but then, she had never been betrothed to him before, either.

He had not approached her since the betrothal had been set. Maybe he did not know what to say any more than she did. Or maybe he *was* having second thoughts about the betrothal. Her nervousness was extremely apparent.

[Maybe if Mary were home she would come with us.]

She could do anything when Mary was with her.

They passed the cobbler's shop. As she approached, about fifty steps behind her brother and sister, she could see Simon working busily with his hammer on someone's new pair of shoes. Simon is the Rabbi's brother. He noticed her and waved as she walked by.

Simon is tall and slender, just the opposite of his brother. He was also very jovial, whereas, the Rabbi is always so solemn and stern looking that he is was almost scary.

Mary Elizabeth was startled when she saw Rabbi Reuben coming out of the cobbler's shop with a new pair of boots under his arm.

"I am looking forward to your Betrothal Feast on Thursday."

"Thank you, Rabbi; my mother has been working very hard to make sure everything will be just right."

"Ah, yes, she is a wonderful cook. Yes, I imagine she *is* working extremely hard", he emphasized while stroking his beard and then he walked on. You could almost see him salivating with anticipation.

Mary Elizabeth had to hurry because her brother and sister were quite a good distance ahead by now. She had spent too much time conversing with the Rabbi, but felt she must.

Next was the candle maker's shop. It was not opened yet. She could see all of the candles hanging in the window from another days work.

The blacksmith's shop could be heard and smelled for a long way.

Aaron was not much older than Abby. He pretty much ran the shop since his father had been badly burned. Joel went in often, but did not do any work. His hands were badly disfigured. He had been distracted by something outside and turned his head just for a second when his hand touched a piece of hot metal. When he jumped, the other hand was also burned. No one could ever figure out why it happened, but it was a definite disaster for the village. He was the best blacksmith in all of the Galilee. Aaron had learned his father's trade at an early age, as had Abby, and he was busy pounding steel into something. She could not tell what it was going to be, but she knew it would be wonderful.

The large fire was raging from its pit and the stench was almost unbearable. Mary Elizabeth could not understand why anyone would want to be a blacksmith.

It was so noisy inside that Aaron had not noticed Abby and Sarah as they passed by, or even Mary Elizabeth as she passed a moment later.

She decided she had better catch up with her siblings. It might look odd to have her walking behind. She might be less conspicuous if she were walking with them.

As they were passing Mary's house, they saw her sitting at the window. They all waved and walked up to her when she leaned out the window.

"Where are you going?" Mary inquired.

"We are on our way to the bakery to see if the breads will be ready for the Betrothal Feast on Thursday night. Would you like to come?"

Sarah had barely gotten the words out of her mouth when Mary Elizabeth broke in, "Please come with us. I am so nervous I cannot go alone."

"But Sarah and Abby are here. You are not alone", replied Mary.

"I know, but I would feel much better if you were with us. Please, Mary, I am sure it would be easier for me if you were there."

"Let me ask my mother. If I am able to go with you I will be right out", Mary said as she moved away from the window.

"I thought you did not want to come", Abby said sarcastically to his older sister, although, she was not much older.

"I was not going to…but I had to. I am so confused I do not have the slightest idea what I am doing."

The three of them waited patiently for Mary. Soon she appeared at the doorway.

"Thanks be to Jehovah! I have no idea what to say or how to act when I see John. How can I speak to him? I am sure all of my words will come out jumbled. I feel so uncomfortable. At this moment, I feel like a child who is just beginning to walk. I just know I am going to fall over my own two feet. I will fall flat on my face and make a fool of myself. What am I going to do?" Mary Elizabeth was talking so fast that it was hard to understand her.

As the four of them were walking, they passed the carpenter's shop. Joseph was not there yet. The shop was still closed.

Mary Elizabeth was hoping he would be working. She wanted to prove to her friend that he would notice her.

Mary was visibly disappointed. She wanted to see for herself if he would see her walking by as Mary Elizabeth had said. Oh well, there would be another time.

Finally they arrived at the bakery. As they entered, Mary Elizabeth sighed in relief, John was not there. However, Joseph's younger sister was. She turned when she heard footsteps behind her.

"Good morning, Mary Elizabeth." She totally ignored the others. Evidently, she had not heard anything about Joseph wanting to ask for Mary's hand or she probably would have addressed her.

"Good morning, Hannah. How are you? I have not seen you for some time", Mary Elizabeth answered.

"I have been very busy helping my mother. I understand you are having a Betrothal Feast soon."

"Yes, Thursday. Father sent us here to make sure the breads will be ready", Mary Elizabeth said.

"My mother has been asked to help. Our whole family is looking forward to it", Hannah remarked.

"I was sorry to hear that your father has been ill. I hope he will be better soon", Mary said with genuine concern in her voice.

"Yes he has been ill. It is not anything serious, though. I guess it is the same ailment that has been going through the entire village. He should be better before the Feast...see you soon.

"Oh, Mary, I hope your father will feel better soon also", she said with sincerity.

⧉

The illness that was 'going through the village' did not go away as quickly as everyone had hoped. The people with the malady had a cough that was deep within the chest. They also had chills and, therefore, had to have blankets put on them to keep them warm.

⧉

Benjamin was behind the long table, on which were many different loaves of bread. The scent of freshly baked goods was usually something to behold, but today it was almost nauseating to Mary Elizabeth. She was definitely getting nervous.

Benjamin Levi was a "portly" gentleman with a jolly laugh that made everyone smile and feel at ease in his presence. This morning Mary Elizabeth did not feel at ease at all. She could feel his eyes on her. She just wanted to get out of there as quickly as possible.

What was he thinking? Was he wondering if she would be a good wife for his son? It was irritating just to have him ogle her as if she were some new kind of tantalizing bread just carried fresh from the oven.

"Oh, Mary Elizabeth, tell your mother that the breads will be ready early Thursday and that I will have my sons deliver them by mid-morning", Benjamin stated before Abby had had time to think how to ask him.

"Thank you. Mother asked me to inquire about the rye", replied Abby as they turned to leave. He wanted the baker to recognize him as the man in charge.

42

"The rye will be ready also." Benjamin was well aware of Abraham's love for his special dark bread and was pleased with his ability to make such a delicacy.

After they left the shop, Abby looked angrily at Mary Elizabeth, "Why did he speak to you instead of me? After all, I am the man here and you are nothing but a girl."

"Just because you had your Bar Mitzvah last month does not mean you are a man to him *or* to me. You are still one of our father's younger children."

"I am a man, I am a man", Abby protested as he stomped on the ground with both feet.

The girls just laughed. It was obvious to them that he was not acting like a man.

"I know why he addressed Mary Elizabeth", Mary said with a big grin from ear to ear. It was not that obvious to the rest, they just looked at her.

"It was because he was recognizing her as his future daughter." Mary Elizabeth blushed.

After they left the store, John appeared, "Whew!" He mopped his brow on his apron, "that was a close one. I thought for sure Mary Elizabeth would see me."

"What is the problem? You will be marrying her in about a year. Are you going to hide from her till then? Benjamin asked brusquely.

"No, Father, I just did not know what to say. This business of being betrothed is new to me. I am not sure how I should act.

When Abby and the girls passed the carpenter's shop again they could see Joseph working. However, he did not see them. He seemed to be very engrossed in whatever it was that he was doing.

"I am sure your father was wrong about Joseph", Mary stated frankly. "If he were interested in me I think I would know. He did not even notice I was walking by."

"Why worry about it?" Mary Elizabeth said, "There will be many more times.

"You have had a lot on your mind lately. It must be hard having your father so ill", Abby said trying to divert her attention.

"Yes it is, but he seems to be getting better each day now. He ate supper with us night before last for the first time in weeks. Mother is busy all the time trying to make him comfortable."

"I am sure he will be better soon. Well, here we are", Sarah said as they stopped in front of Mary's house.

"I am really glad that you invited me to go with you", Mary said as she walked toward her door.

"Thank you for going, even if John was not there after all. It was nice having your company", Abby said.

[Abby is always such a polite boy. Mama and Papa have done an excellent job of raising him. He seems to have more compassion than most boys his age. It is a pleasure having him for a brother, although it is fun to tease him. I think he thought when he had his Bar Mitzvah he would become a man instantly. I enjoy telling him he is still a child.

He does know how to work hard. Father taught him while he was young how to properly care for sheep. Someday, when he really is a man and wants to be married, Father will give him a few ewes and a ram and maybe a couple of lambs so he can start his own herd. He will be a fine shepherd.]

༅

That night Mary Elizabeth had a very fretful sleep. She had had many dreams in her life, but nothing like this. She tossed and turned for hours after waking up. She just could not understand why she would dream something like that. What did it mean?

She would not be able to tell it to her mother or father. They would think she was deranged or demented or just plain daft. But she would have to tell someone. This seemed too important to keep something like this to herself.

She would tell Mary. Yes, she could tell Mary anything, after all, they were like sisters. Maybe she would not know the meaning of the dream, either, but at least she would not berate her for being strange or demented or daft. Yes, she would tell Mary. That was the only alternative she could come up with.

She lay awake until dawn thinking of the possible explanations for the dream. It was so vivid, as if she were there and knew to whom the event was happening. How could that be? She did not recognize the persons or anyone else around. Even the setting and the area were not recognizable. But then, she had never been far from Nazareth; this seemed to be a great distance away. The terrain was unfamiliar. She did not know how she could tell, however, but that was the way it seemed. There *was* a familiarity about the people in the dream she could not explain.

Finally, she could see the sky getting lighter. She would get up soon.

As dawn came and the first cock crowed, she was up and dressed. She went to the cooking area where her mother was just starting the morning meal.

"What brings you out so early, Daughter? I was just about to call you", Theresa exclaimed. "What about Sarah? Is she up, too?"

"She is still sleeping. I did not want to disturb her, I could not sleep. I awoke in the night after I had had a dream. After that my sleep would not return. I lay awake the rest of the night just thinking."

"What was your dream about?" Abraham was up and hearing the conversation, joined in.

"It was of no importance. I really do not even know who the people were in the dream. It was very strange to me because I could see people but not faces. The faces were blurry. No one was recognizable."

"You have really got me wondering. What was happening to the people? Please, tell me about it", Abraham said anxiously.

"Not now, Papa. I would like to think about it for a while."

"Come, Mary Elizabeth, we had better fix the meal so that your father and Abby can be off to the sheep pens."

⥲•⥳

With the house straightened and Theresa busily baking and making preparations for the Feast, Mary Elizabeth quietly slipped out of the house and made her way to Mary's.

45

Retrieving a bucket for water made the perfect excuse to get away, not that she had fooled her mother.

It was almost mid-morning by this time and she was sure that her friend would be able to spend some time with her.

To her surprise, Mary was at the well when she arrived.

"Mary, I am so glad to see you. I have been thinking about you all morning."

"I have been thinking about you, too. I awoke with a start in the middle of the night and had the feeling that we should talk. I could not get back to sleep. I have been worried about you ever since."

"That is really strange because I have had the feeling that you were the only one that I could talk to", Mary Elizabeth iterated.

"My father wanted me to tell him, but I just did not feel it was the right thing to do. It seemed so real to me that I feel as though he would make light of it and it seemed so profound."

"What are you talking about?" her friend asked, "Mary, I have had a dream, a very real dream. I cannot explain it. I do not have a clue as to what it might mean."

"Tell me. Hurry! I cannot wait to hear it. It must be something important or I would not have woken up at the precise moment you dreamed your dream."

"You better take your bucket of water home first. Your mother might be waiting for it. I will draw my water and take it home and then we will meet at the 'rock'.

"All right, I will be waiting there for you", Mary said.

&⊶⋞

The 'rock' was where Mary Elizabeth and Mary had played as children. It stands in sight of the highway, but just far enough away that no one ever bothered them. There they would pretend to be wives and mothers, teaching their ill-fashioned babies the things that their mothers had taught them. As the years passed, they continued to meet there to talk about things that only the best of friends and sisters could talk about.

Their mothers were good friends, too. They had been since Mary's birth. And the two Mary's had been best friends since they were old enough to look at each other and 'coo'.

❧∞❧

When Mary Elizabeth arrived, Mary was waiting for her.

"Well, tell me, Mary Elizabeth. I cannot bare the waiting. I feel I shall burst if you do not tell me right away."

Mary Elizabeth had never seen such excitement in Mary the whole time she had known her.

"Let me tell it slowly, so that I do not leave out any of the details."

She took a deep breath and dug deep into her brain to recall it all.

"In my dream", she drew in another deep breath and let it out slowly, "it was night and the moon was shining brightly."

Then she continued, "Next I saw a great light. I knew it was night, but the light was so bright it looked as if it was noonday."

Then it occurred to me that it was a great star. It was the biggest star I have ever seen", she opened her arms as wide as she was able, to demonstrate the size. Then she elaborated, "None of the other stars compared to it in size or brilliance. It was shining especially bright in one particular spot; on a small town. I did not recognize the town.

But I could tell that it was not Nazareth. I do know that".

She stopped to take in another deep breath and to let it out slowly once again while collecting her thoughts. "I know that sounds peculiar, but that is what I saw."

Mary did not say a word, she just listened intently.

"I also saw what looked like shepherds walking toward the star. I knew they were shepherds because they each held a staff in their hand. They seemed to be following the star. As they walked, they were looking up. They walked slowly, but steady. I had the feeling that they were curious to see what wonderful thing the star was leading them to and why it was shining on the town."

She waited a few seconds before starting again. "Mary, it was so real. Just outside of the town there was a cave, no, it was a stable. Actually, it was a cave made into a stable. There were many animals inside. There was a man and a woman inside. I could not see their faces. I could not see who they were, but I felt I should know them.

"The woman was lying on some hay and the man was sitting next to her wiping her brow with a damp cloth.

"Toward the back of the stable there was a manger." Another long pause, "Mary, in the manger a baby was laying. I am sure it was a boy. I *could* see his face. His was the only face that was recognizable. He was beautiful and he lay so peaceful. He looked like he should be a king, but he was not dressed like a king. He had on clean cloths wrapped tightly about his small little body. I wanted to cry. I wanted to go and get him some fine clothes to wear; clothes befitting a king.

"I felt so sorry that he had to have a manger for his bed. It seemed so terrible, but at the same time it was all so wonderful. I wanted to be there, to hold that precious baby in my arms. Then I awoke."

Mary looked at her friend; she seemed mesmerized by the whole situation.

"What could all of this mean, Mary? I really want to know. I am very troubled by the whole thing."

"I wish I knew, but I really do not", Mary said sullenly.

She hesitated for a few minutes trying to bring back to her memory something they had learned as children.

"We were taught that there would be a bright star that would show the way to Bethlehem where the Messiah is to be born."

"Yes, but…in a stable?"

"I really do not know. You know that he is to be born of a virgin maiden named Mary and that he will be a Nazarene. Maybe you are to be his mother and you are getting a glimpse into the future."

"But the town did not look like Nazareth. And besides your name is Mary, too. Most of the maidens I know are named Mary, at least in some part of their name. Why would I be the mother of the Messiah?"

Mary looked thoughtfully at Mary Elizabeth and then said, "Why not? You are a virgin. You are worthy. He will be born of the line of David and you are of that lineage. Yes, why not you?" she said confidently.

"Oh, Mary, do you think it might be possible?" Mary Elizabeth said with renewed enthusiasm.

"Anything is possible with Jehovah.

Mary was pleased that she could reveal these things to Mary Elizabeth. She would make a wonderful mother and an honorable one for the Messiah.

Mary Elizabeth was glad that she had been able to tell Mary about her dream. She felt so much better.

છ⊷જ

The description of the Sabbath ceremony was found in "Two From Galilee" by Marjorie Holmes pp. 56, 57, & 58.

In Biblical times, the father of the groom paid the father of the bride a price for the privilege of his daughter. This was because the bride would leave her father's house and go to live with her husband. Her father would lose a worker and the groom would gain one. "Celebrating Life: Jewish rites of Passage" by Malka Drucker pp. 50 & 51

The account of the star, shepherds, etc. was taken from the New Testament KJV, Luke Chapter 2

CHAPTER
FOUR

Thursday came with a bang…literally, thunder, lightning and torrential rain all day long.

[This has to be a bad omen. How could there be a Betrothal Feast in the rain. Maybe it should be cancelled. Maybe John and I are not supposed to be married. I must not keep having such thoughts. Everything will be fine.]

The tents had been put up Wednesday night before the rain had started so, at least, the floor would be dry. The carpets had been laid and the curtains draped. It looked wonderful.

Two of Benjamin Levi's sons had delivered the breads however, John was not one of them. But then that would not have been proper. Still, Mary Elizabeth thought he might have come to see his bride-to-be.

She still had not seen him since the Sabbath. She was hoping all was well with him. It worried her that he had not come to her house to see her after some evening meal. With both of her parents there, they would have been sufficiently chaperoned.

She had not been able to talk to Mary that day. She had been much too busy helping her mother with last minute preparations.

Some of the men in the village were roasting the lambs. Mary Elizabeth's father had picked only the best lambs and he and Abby had dressed, seasoned them and were watching them with intent as they roasted.

Today, it was Sarah's job to fetch water and add finishing touches to the tents as requested by her mother and also to milk the goat.

Abby was busy helping Abraham do whatever else was necessary for a Betrothal Feast. Best of all was staying out of the women's way.

About sundown, all of the preparations were ready and it had quit raining. Mary Elizabeth was dressed in the gown her mother had used for her own Betrothal Feast and it fit her perfectly. She looked beautiful and felt it, too. Sarah was doting on her like a mother hen, but Mary Elizabeth did not mind, in fact she was enjoying it immensely. Now all she could do was wait for the festivities to begin.

She would not be allowed at the feast until it was well under way. She could hear the music and longed to be there, but knew she had to wait for just the right time.

Right now the men were dancing, singing and telling jokes about wedding night horrors in order to embarrass John.

Mary appeared at the door to stay with Mary Elizabeth until the time for her appearance.

"Are you ready, Mary Elizabeth?" Mary turned the girl around slowly and looked her all over. "You look beautiful. I have never seen you look so radiant."

"I am *sooo* nervous. I feel like I have horse flies rumbling around in my stomach. I really do not know if I am ready for this. Hold my hands and tell me that everything will be all right."

Mary took both of the girl's hands in her own and they sat down on the straw mattress.

"You know this is what you have always wanted. John is the man of your dreams. You are the one he chose. Besides, we are sisters; you know I will always be there for you."

"Have you seen John tonight?"

"Yes, he is more handsome than I have ever seen him. And he seems to be having a wonderful time."

"Mama, is it time to leave yet?" Mary Elizabeth enquired while her whole body shook with nervousness.

"Just about, Daughter, be patient."

Finally, the time had arrived for Mary Elizabeth to make her entrance. All the women of the town walked to the tent and entered making a walkway for the bride.

Everyone "Oohed and Ahhd" as Mary Elizabeth entered the tent. Her mother's dress was perfect and her face glowed with a brilliance that John had never seen before in any woman. He knew at once that he had made the right choice. Mary Elizabeth was, to him, the most beautiful woman he had ever known and would be the perfect wife. After all, Theresa *was* her mother and everyone knew what a wonderful wife, housekeeper, cook and mother she was. Tutored at her knee, she would have to be perfect.

As Mary Elizabeth entered there were nods of admiration for John's choice for his mate. She was seated next to John. As she gazed into his eyes she could feel the love he had for her.

The Betrothal Ceremony, officiated by Rabbi Reuben, was beautiful. He did not seem as stern as Mary Elizabeth had remembered.

The scribe was called forward. It was his duty to write down all of the covenants that were made by the couple. The covenants would then be given to the bride and groom at the time of their wedding, so that they would always remember them.

The Rabbi nodded to John to let him know that it was time for him and Mary Elizabeth to come forth. John gently took his bride by the hand and led her to the front of the tent. Mary Elizabeth was not her usual self. At this moment she was very quiet and reserved. She was enjoying this solemn time with reverence.

Then the Rabbi asked John, "Have you brought a token to give to the bride to show that this covenant is made?"

John unwound his girdle, which had the money sack in it and handed it to the Rabbi, who then placed it in Mary Elizabeth's hands, which were held high above her head.

"And have you other gifts?"

"I have", John replied, as he fumbled for a handmade basket which he handed to Theresa. Then he handed a new pair of sandals to Abraham. Then both nodded their approval.

Next, he handed Mary Elizabeth a shawl hand-made by his mother and the small, carved box which was hand tooled by Joseph. And last of all, a beautiful hand-carved mirror which he had purchased last time he was in Jerusalem. He knew it would be the perfect gift for his Betrothed.

She had never had a mirror of her own. She had used her mother's, but this one was hers alone. She sat a moment and stared into the beautiful gift.

Then he made a statement looking directly into his brides' eyes, "I will love you, honor you and work for you all the days of my life and everything I own or will ever own will be yours also forever".

The scribe wrote all the words down so it would be remembered always.

After, John draped Mary Elizabeth's face with the betrothal veil. With this done, the children were called forward to receive their cakes and candies. This was done to symbolize that she had kept herself pure for him.

Then Rabbi Reuben gave the happy couple another blessing. He told each of them how fortunate they were to have each other and that they should treasure one another forever. Somehow, they both knew that it would be so.

They were definitely in love. They had loved each other secretly for a long time. In some marriages arranged by parents, the couple has to fall in love after the marriage. Sometimes they never do and spend a lifetime just tolerating each other. Heaven forbid! In this marriage, that will not be the case. Their love can only grow stronger with each ensuing year.

Now it was official, they belonged to each other.

&∘&

A Betrothal Contract is just as binding as the Marriage Contract. In fact, if one or both of them should change their minds or if there is a transgression, there had to be a bill of divorcement in order to break the contract. Surely that would never happen to them.

&∘&

The Feast was a great success, as everyone knew it would be.

Everyone had a wonderful time. The food was delicious. There was plenty with some left over, just as it should be. The wine flowed all night. There seemed to be no end to it.

53

Mary was there, of course, with her family even though the Feast was for John and Mary Elizabeth, she felt very much a part of it all. Her father was feeling much better, but she was not surprised when he left early. She knew he would not want to over-exert himself.

Where had Joseph gone? Mary knew he had been there earlier. There were so many people maybe she just had not seen him. That was silly. How could she miss him? He was all that she had thought of day and night since Mary Elizabeth and her own mother had talked about him.

Maybe he had not had such a good time or maybe he had some pressing business that had to be taken care of which could not wait until morning. Joseph was such a conscientious person.

Everyone had eaten and danced until dawn. John and Mary Elizabeth had a wonderful time and could hardly take their eyes off one another. Yes, everything was perfect.

꩜

"Mary Elizabeth", Came the shout of excitement at her window. "Mary Elizabeth, are you awake?"

"Ummmm, Ohhh, why must you awaken me so early? You must know that I was up until early this morning. All that dancing has made me so tired. Come back later today. I want to...slee..." Mary went to the front door and knocked hard and rapid.

Theresa answered, "Mary, is everything all right?"

"Yes, I just want to see Mary Elizabeth."

"I am sorry, Dear, she is still sleeping."

"Please, believe me, she will not mind", came the reply.

Mary hurried to the girl's room where she said angrily, "Mary Elizabeth! I thought we were sisters. I have some news. It will not wait", Mary continued in an excited tone.

Mary Elizabeth sat straight up in her bed. She had never heard her friend raise her voice. She was definitely wide awake now.

"Oh, Mary Elizabeth, I am so thrilled I can hardly believe it."

"Mary, will you please tell me what you are talking about?"

54

"Joseph asked for my hand last night." Mary almost swooned as she thought about the whole event. She fell straight back on the bed and lay there musing and said nothing more for what seemed like an eternity.

"Mary! What are you telling me? Joseph actually got up the courage to have his father ask your father for your hand? How did that happen?"

"I guess during your feast Joseph decided it was the right time. I noticed he was not there, but I did not know why. I guess he was talking to his father at that time. He must have gone home after that.

"My father was not there either, but I figured he was tired and had gone home early. He is still not completely well."

Mary arose from her prone position and the two hugged tightly.

"I can hardly believe it. We will both be married around the same time. That will be wonderful", her friend blurted out. "It seems we are sisters in everything we do."

"Have you spoken with Joseph since the two fathers spoke?"

"Yes, but only for a brief moment", Mary confided.

"Well?" Mary Elizabeth was motioning for more information.

"My father came back to the tent and took me aside to tell me that Joseph wants to marry me. Well, Joseph was waiting for Mama and me as we came out of the tent to go home. As we walked toward home he said he was very happy that we would be marrying sometime next year and that he would do all he could to be a good husband. I responded by telling him I would be the best wife any man ever had.

"Oh, it was all so romantically wonderful." Her eyes twinkled as brilliantly as a million stars in the sky.

"I told you that it was just a matter of time before he would ask for your hand. You are the only possible one for him. I cannot wait to tell Papa and Mama. I am so excited for you that I can hardly breathe", Mary Elizabeth said as she clutched the left side of her chest with her right hand.

"And I thought I was the only one who was having trouble breathing. It feels as if I have a camel sitting on my chest", Mary jokingly chuckled.

"When will you have your Betrothal Feast?"

"I am not sure. My father has not said anything about the arrangements. I *am* sure it will be soon. First the announcement has to be made in the Synagogue."

"It would be such fun to have a double wedding. How do you feel about that?" Mary Elizabeth said dramatically.

"I would love that, too. We could do everything together. We could get our mothers together and help them with all of the planning. I think it would be exciting for our mothers, too. Just imagine, we could plan all of the food and help make it. We could help decorate for the Wedding Feast. Maybe we could make matching wedding gowns", Mary interjected with added enthusiasm.

"We had better talk to our parents this evening and let them know of our plans."

⊱⊰

Joseph entered the bakery. He decided to let his father open the carpentry shop this morning.

"Why are you open so early?" Joseph asked Benjamin.

"Work goes on whether we sleep or not. What happened to you last night? I saw you for a little while, but then you were gone", Benjamin remarked.

John, having an idea what had happened said, "Tell me all about it".

"There is not much to tell", Joseph was having a hard time keeping a straight face. "My father asked Jacob for Mary's hand", he stated matter-of-factly.

John walked up to Joseph and slapped him on the back hard, nearly knocking him over, "I knew you could do it. But where did *you* go?"

"Home, I was so nervous that I knew I would not be much fun to be around."

Changing the subject, "What are you doing up so early, John? Would your father not let you sleep?"

"Who could sleep? It was such a glorious night I never wanted it to be over. I imagine Mary Elizabeth will sleep a long time."

"I doubt that. I think Mary will be over there very early", Joseph said with confidence.

"It must have been very late when Jacob told Mary. I would think she would want to sleep awhile", Benjamin commented.

"Knowing Mary, she will not be able to sleep. She will want to tell Mary Elizabeth first thing this morning. You know those two, they tell each other everything. John, I think you had better build your house next to ours. Better yet, I should make ours a little bigger and you can move right in with us", Joseph said teasing.

The men laughed and then John said, "No, thank you, I see enough of you now. I would not want to live with you, too. I cannot imagine waking up to your ugly face every morning. I do not even think I want to live next to you."

Now they were laughing so hard that Benjamin had tears running down his face. John and Joseph, seeing that, laughed all the harder.

When things settled down John asked, "Did you speak with Mary after the meeting?"

"Yes, but just for a couple of minutes. The Feast was just breaking up. Mary and her mother were walking home.

"Naomi walked a little behind us so that we could talk. I walked her to her door and said 'Goodnight'. That was about all."

John had another question that was bothering him. "Did you talk to her about building your home near their rock?"

"I think that is a little premature. We have not even had the announcement in the Synagogue. I will soon, though."

❧◦❦

"Papa, you were right. Joseph has asked for Mary's hand. I knew he would be the one. They are so suited for each other", Mary Elizabeth said passionately. "They will be married about the same

57

time as John and I. Maybe we will have a double wedding", she stated cautiously. She was not sure how that statement would be received.

"No, I will not allow that!" her mother screamed hysterically, "I want your wedding to be special. If you are married in a double ceremony it will not be special to you. And besides, I will have to share the honor with Naomi."

"Mama, I love you very much, but Mary is my best friend, and I think it would be wonderful if we could have a double wedding. And just think, you would only have half of the work of preparation", Mary Elizabeth suggested, trying to tempt her mother into seeing things her way.

"Well, maybe John and Joseph will not want it that way. Have either of you talked to them? You really should consult the bridegrooms on such important decisions, you know", Abraham added.

"No, I had not thought about that", the daughter said wistfully. "I did not think it would mean that much to either of them, after all, they are good friends, too. All I thought about was how much fun it would be for Mary and me. I guess I *have* been selfish. I will talk to John tomorrow."

⧯

That night Mary Elizabeth had another dream. Again it woke her with a start and again it puzzled her.

She could not understand why this was happening to her. Why was she having these dreams? What did they mean? Or did they mean anything at all? Maybe it was just some nightmare that she could not control.

She would talk to Mary about it in the morning, but now she needed sleep. But sleep would not come. She turned this way and that way. She stood up and looked out the window at the moon. It looked especially bright tonight. She thought she could see a face on the surface of it. It seemed to be smiling at her. What secret did it hold behind those dark spots? What did it know that she did not? Was it laughing at her because she was so confused or because of her not knowing the mysteries of life? Or was the moon trying to

58

tell her something foreboding? Was Jehovah conveying some hidden message to her? Or was it an angel that was sending messages through her dreams.

She lay back on her bed and tossed and turned until the cock crowed again.

Mary Elizabeth arrived at Mary's house about mid-day. All of her chores had been done. This was the usual time of day that she tried to find time to spend with her best friend.

Mary was still straightening the house for her mother.

"My mother was not very happy about the prospects of having a double wedding", Mary Elizabeth said. She was talking softly so that Mary's mother would not hear the conversation.

"Neither was mine. Maybe we should forget the whole thing", Mary stated emphatically.

"Do we really want to? I still think it would be wonderful. I would really like us to be a part of each other's wedding. We have always played a big part in each other's lives. Why should we change that now?"

"I agree. We should be able to have our weddings our way", Mary giggled.

"We forgot some very important people when we were planning to have a double wedding."

"Who did we forget?" Mary asked inquisitively.

"What if John and Joseph will not want a double wedding? We really need to ask what they want", answered Mary Elizabeth.

"You are right. I wish I had thought of that", Mary exclaimed. "I'll talk to Joseph today as soon as my mother has time to go with me."

"I'll get my mother to go with me this evening so that I will be properly chaperoned", Mary Elizabeth said as she rolled her eyes. "You know that it would not be proper to be with the men alone", she said with sarcasm, "I hope they will agree to it."

"I do not understand why we cannot be alone together. After all, we are going to be married."

"Mary Elizabeth, I cannot believe you said that", Mary said shocked. "You know how people would talk if we were seen alone with our Betroths."

"I know, but I still think it is silly. I will make sure my mother goes with me.

"But first, I have something else to talk to you about." Mary Elizabeth's demeanor had turned quite somber.

"Mary, it happened again last night."

Mary stopped what she was doing and sat on the bed. "Do you want to go to the rock to talk?"

"Would you mind?"

"NO, if it would make you feel more comfortable. Let me tell Mother", Mary said intuitively.

When she returned she stated, "Mother said I need to be back in about an hour. I still have more things that need to be done."

Mary's mother knew that when the girls needed to be alone that they retreated to their special place on the outskirts of he village.

Mary Elizabeth purposely took her time walking to the rock. She did not say a word the whole way, which was extremely unusual, so Mary did not try to hurry her along. She knew that her friend was troubled by something. She also knew that she would talk when she was ready.

They both stood on top of this extraordinary spot and let the wind blow through their clothes. Mary carefully unwrapped the shawl from off her shoulders and then from off her head. Mary Elizabeth removed her veil. No one would see her. They let their hair fly every which way; something they had often done as children. It had been so wonderful to be carefree and young.

In the distance they could see a caravan approaching the village to buy supplies for another leg of their journey and also to sell some of their wares. Perhaps they might even stay at the Inn tonight.

≈•≈

As children, they had pretended that they were princesses on a caravan going to the some far away castle to marry handsome princes.

Now, both of them were marrying the men of their dreams. No, John and Joseph were not princes and the girls were not princesses.

The games had been fun, but this was real. Still, they were contented with where they were in life.

Soon they sat down, took their sandals off and with their arms wrapped tightly around their knees, watched as the caravan approached. Where was it going? What hidden treasures were upon the camel's backs? Were the men, riding the camels, sultans, kings, or just merchants.

It was much more exciting pretending they might be kings than just common merchants. They had seen many merchants, but they had never seen a king.

What far distant land did they come from; perhaps Babylon, or Greece, or even Gaul.

What was their destination? Was it Jerusalem or possibly the mysterious East?

Pretending had been exciting when they were children, but they were no longer children. They must put away things of their childhood and think as women.

❧❧

Finally, Mary Elizabeth spoke, "Mary, I have had another dream. It was totally different from the first one.

"I am worried. I want to know why I am having these dreams. Why me? They are so disturbing. Once dream is over...so is my sleep. I lay there to think about my night vision."

"Tell me about it, Mary Elizabeth", her best friend said solemnly.

Mary Elizabeth just sat quiet, looking out over the vast horizon, trying to put the dream into words that might make sense.

"Last night I saw a large building. I think it must have been the Temple in Jerusalem. I cannot think what else it would have been, even though I have never seen the Temple. The reason I knew it was the Temple was the way it was adorned. It was beautiful; more beautiful than any of our Synagogues. And it was much larger.

"There was a boy, about Abby's age. He wore a Yarmulke. He seemed to be talking to the men. There were many men in a circle and the boy was in the middle. The men were not angry or chastising the boy. They seemed to be listening very intently like the boy was teaching them something.

Mary Elizabeth snickered to herself and then said, "I know that boys do not teach men, but that seemed to be what was happening. The men were drawn into what the boy had to say. There were people coming from all directions in the Temple to hear him.

"Next, two people, a man and a woman, seemed to be reprimanding the boy. However, he did not seem to care. I do not know if he was being chastened because he was teaching the men or for some other reason. That was all. That was the end of my dream.

"Oh, Mary, I feel that if I do not find out what this is all about I will go mad. It really bothers me."

"Well, I sure do not know what to make of it. Maybe it is he the Messiah teaching in the Temple."

"But he was only a boy. How could that be?"

"Yes, but you must remember, the last time you saw him he was a baby. He must grow up, he surely cannot stay a baby and he should not be able to go from being a baby to a man. There must be a child in between. Also the Messiah is the Son of God. Who is to say that he would not or could not teach in the Temple at such a young age? It is strange, though, that he would be teaching grown men. Why not teaching other children his own age?"

"Oh, Mary, what am I to do? I have to stop this dreaming. I am so tired from the sleep I have lost. I am exhausted from all of the thinking that goes along with the lack of sleep. My body has a hard time just doing the things that have to be done.

"I wonder if I should tell John about my dreams."

"Not yet. Maybe we should think on this some more and try to come up with some logical reasoning behind the dreams", Mary ventured.

Mary put her shawl back over her head, Mary Elizabeth replaced her veil. They both put their sandals back on and returned to the village and watched as the caravan approached. It was a marvelous sight to behold.

But sorrow crept upon the girls as they realized there were no Kings or Queens or Sultans or even Princes; only merchants.

There were about fifteen camels with only about six men walking beside them, two camel drivers and four merchants. There was merchandise piled and covered high upon the camel's backs.

The girls' mothers also knew that the caravan had arrived. News travels fast in small villages. They were both anticipating looking at their wares, as were all of the other women in the village.

They must have wonderful items that they would like to sell; beautiful cloths, spices, perfume scented body oils. Rugs, yes, Persian rugs, they must have many of those. What wonderful treasures to behold. Maybe they would even have new pots for cooking and much, much more. But the women would not be able to buy anything until the camels were in large pens, fed and watered. The camel drivers would do that.

The merchants needed to be settled at one of the Inns after they had eaten a scrumptious meal of mutton, roasted vegetables, big slabs of bread with honey, cheese and many mugs of wine. Then they would be expected to rest for a while so that they would have the energy to withstand all of the haggling that would take place.

After an appropriate amount of time had passed they would spread blankets on the ground and lay out their commodities and wait for the men to come home before any purchasing could be done.

Because these were strangers, the women were not allowed to purchase anything from the vendors. They could go with the men, look and pick out any items they might be interested in purchasing. However, they must not look too anxious, because it was the job of the men to haggle over the price. And if they looked like they really wanted an item the traders would not bring the price down as low as the purchasers thought it should be.

The merchant would look back and forth from the husband to the wife trying to read their faces. The wife must not look the least bit eager or she might spoil the whole transaction. Eventually, the goods would be sold. This took long hours because the haggling would be done for each item that was wanted. And the buyers were relentless when it came to haggling.

If an agreement would not be made, the purchaser would pretend to walk away until the merchant would call him back to haggle some more. It was a great game. The merchants and the purchasers enjoyed the festivities far too much.

The children could not go near to the merchandise. They had to wait until the episode was finished.

Then the purchases were made and the families would return to their homes. The men would brag about how shrewd they had been, not realizing that the merchants had asked for unholy prices because they knew that there would be heated arguments until the prices were brought down to where they should have been in the first place.

♊⁃♂

When Mary Elizabeth got home, her mother could see that something was wrong.

"What has happened? You do not look like the happy bride anymore. Did you have a misunderstanding with Mary? What can make you look like this?"

"I'm fine. I have just been having some weird dreams lately. I do not know the meaning of them and they worry me."

"Mary Elizabeth, tell me of your dreams. I worry when I see you like this", Theresa stated.

"Mama, I am afraid you will think something is wrong with me and, well, maybe there is.

"I have told my dreams to Mary. She has tried to interpret them for me, but I am still confused."

"I have some time now, please tell the dreams to me", her mother insisted still worried about her oldest child.

Mary Elizabeth proceeded to tell about the two dreams she had had and the interpretation that Mary had given her.

"That has to be it", Theresa exclaimed with joy, "You are to be the mother of the Messiah.

"Just think...you are the 'Chosen One'. We have been waiting for this event for generations, and my child is the one who is to give birth to the Messiah.

"I knew we had done the right thing when we named you Mary. I know Jehovah inspired us", Theresa exclaimed as the enthusiasm mounted in the woman's voice.

"Mama, calm down. We do not know that this is the right interpretation. Maybe there is another explanation for my having these dreams.

"Please do not tell *anyone* these things" Mary Elizabeth begged.

"I must tell your father, but I promise I will tell no one else", Theresa pledged.

That evening Theresa and Mary Elizabeth walked to the bakery just about the time it was to close. John was cleaning the last table and was about to clean the floor when the women entered.

"John, Mary Elizabeth would like to speak to you", Theresa said.

"Everything is all right, I hope", Benjamin commented concerned.

"Everything is fine, Father Benjamin. I just want to discuss something with John, if it is all right", Mary Elizabeth answered softly.

John motioned for the women to follow him into the back room so they could have some privacy.

When they were there, Mary Elizabeth began speaking, "John, we will be getting married about the same time as Mary and Joseph. Mary and I thought it would be nice to have a double wedding.

John looked thoughtfully as his espoused continued, "There are many advantages to having a double wedding. It would be less expense for our parents. It would also be less work for our mothers.

About this time Theresa interjected, "But I am looking forward to the work. A mother waits a lifetime for her daughter to be married. I want to do it by myself.

John, being diplomatic, said, "I understand your feelings, Mother Theresa, and I also understand Mary Elizabeth's. It would not be taking the glory away from you. Just think, the wedding would be twice as grand with both mothers working together.

"And it makes more sense to have one big wedding instead of two.

"Yes, I think it would be very wise to do it Mary Elizabeth and Mary's way. Think of the splendor."

John put his arms around the shoulders of the two women as he guided them toward the front door. "I think it is a wonderful suggestion and I am sure with your efforts it will be the best wedding ever seen in Nazareth."

Both women went home satisfied. Mary Elizabeth had gotten her way and Theresa was dreaming of how wonderful the wedding would be with her and Naomi working together.

Joseph had agreed to the double wedding and the girls were ecstatic.

⧉

The Betrothal Ceremony was taken from "Two From Galilee" by Marjorie Holmes pp. 67, 68 and 69.

The dream of the Temple was taken from The New Testament KJV, Luke Chapter 2 vs. 46-49

CHAPTER FIVE

"Yes, Benjamin, Mary Elizabeth is to be the 'Chosen One'. Our grandson will be The Messiah", Abraham bragged.

"How do you know this?" Benjamin returned as he was kneading the whole wheat bread.

"Mary Elizabeth has been having dreams. The dreams told her that she is to bare the 'Awaited One'.

"Think of it. You and I will be the grandparents of God's Son. We are truly blessed", Abraham reaffirmed. "Theresa and I are so proud, as you should be also. If John had not chosen my Mary Elizabeth, you would not be the grandfather of The Messiah."

Benjamin put the loaf on the table to rise one more time and asked, "Are you sure of what you speak?"

"Of course, Theresa told me herself just today. But please do not tell a soul. I was not supposed to tell anyone myself, but because you are to be the other grandfather, I thought you should know."

The two men hugged and danced around the bakery, basking in the revelry of the moment.

&∞&

By the time of Joseph's and Mary's Betrothal Feast it was told throughout Galilee that Mary Elizabeth and John were to be the parents of "The Holy One".

Joseph and Mary were happy for the chosen couple and both agreed that their friends would be fine parents for "The Savior of the World".

Exactly one month after Joseph and Mary's Betrothal Feast Mary Elizabeth had another dream. It had been a while since the last one, so she was hoping the last one was the end.

This one concerned a man. The first was about a star and a baby. The second one was about a boy in what she knew must be the Temple in Jerusalem.

Again it happened in the middle of the night. Maybe she *was* to be the Messiah's mother. What other reason could there be for her having these strange dreams.

Was the man in this dream just a man or was he 'The Messiah'? Whichever was the case he was a grown man, handsome, strong and with piercing eyes that seemed to look right into the soul of a person.

As she lay awake after the dream she thought maybe she understood what was happening. For some unknown reason she was seeing the Savior's life. First she saw his birth, then as a young man and last as a full-grown man. Now, maybe, this would be the end of these episodes.

Why she was chosen to have these dreams, she did not understand. Anyway, she knew she had to tell Mary about this one, too.

Again, she could not sleep the rest of the night. She arose and paced the floor, trying to be as quiet as possible. She did not want to arouse Sarah or anyone else who was sleeping.

She groped in the darkness for clothes to put on. She moved something, which immediately fell to the floor with a thud.

She crawled on her hands and knees and swept the floor with her hand until she found the rock that she uses for a paperweight which was lying under the table. She put it back on top. Abby had given the rock to her one day when he had come back from watching the sheep. He thought it was exceptional and wanted to give it to his big sister.

Sarah awoke. "What are you doing?"

"I'm trying to find my clothes", Mary Elizabeth whispered.

"Why? It is still dark outside", came the response.

"Shh", Mary Elizabeth said softly, trying not to make any more noise.

"I know it is still dark, but I cannot sleep. I woke up and now I am wide-awake.

"Did you have another one of your dreams?" Sarah said excitedly.

"Go back to sleep, Sarah".

"May I go with you?"

"No, I need to be alone. I have a lot of thinking to do. I am going to the rock. I can think clearer there. *Alone!* I love you, but I must reason this out in my mind. Please stay here."

"I will, but I know I will not be able to get back to sleep", Sarah stated as she lay back down.

With that Mary Elizabeth was into her clothes and started out the curtain which separated that room from the others.

As she walked through the house, she could hear her father snoring. The soft muffled sound was steady. She knew he would not awaken for a while. She opened the door in the front of the house. It creaked a little. She hoped that no one would hear.

The dog by the door lifted his head and looked but made no sound and again rested his head on his front paws.

Mary Elizabeth hurried past all of the shops in the sleeping little village trying not to make a sound, but the stones on the road crackled beneath her sandals.

She could barely make out the rock in the blackness of the night, but there it was.

When she could touch it, she ran her hands over it in almost a ritualistic way. This rock belonged to Mary and herself. Here was their refuge, their place of safety. She knew she would bother no one and no one would bother her, not even Mary, for she knew that her friend was fast asleep in her own home, oblivious to what was happening to Mary Elizabeth.

Her confidant would be told later, but now she needed to be alone with her thoughts.

She climbed to the top of the rock and sat once more with her arms wrapped tightly around her knees looking into the blackness. This was her favorite position in which to sit on top of *her* rock.

Here she would be able to think and not be disturbed by anyone or disturbing anyone else. She needed to sort things out.

[Am I to be the mother of the Messiah? How am I to know for sure? How would I prepare myself for such a thing? I know that

Mary said I am worthy, but am I really? I must find out. I am sure the mother of God's child should be holy. I am definitely not *holy*. I have many weaknesses. I am selfish. I think mean thoughts…sometimes. I like to tease. I am not always as obedient as I should be]

Mary Elizabeth turned herself toward the East. The sky was just beginning to lighten over a distant hill.

Birds were starting to fly to and fro looking for some succulent morsel to eat and then to fly to a nest somewhere to regurgitate some of it for their babies.

The sun was beginning to peek slowly over the hill as if to say, "I am coming. Everyone, awake and arise. A new day is here. There is much to be done, you had better get started."

Soon the yellow brilliance shone straight into Mary Elizabeth's eyes. It happened so suddenly that it took her by surprise. It looked as if a great ball of saffron fire were emerging from some unknown cavern deep within the earth that had been awakened from a deep sleep and was ready to devour everything in its path.

There were a few clouds which took on a bright yellow tinge around the edges that was brilliant. The sky seemed to erupt into gleaming rays. It was spectacular.

The house that Joseph was building for himself and Mary was beginning to take shape. She had felt a little sad when she found out that Mary's home would be by the rock…*her* rock.

She soon had accepted that. At least it was Mary's rock, too.

She did not know what she would have done if someone else had built a home there.

Now she must run home. Her mother would be fixing the meal and wonder where her eldest daughter had gone so early in the morning.

As she was descending, her foot slipped on one of the loose rocks at the base of the immense protrusion. Not being able to brace herself against the fall, she landed face down with her legs and arms sprawled in every direction. Embarrassed, she got to her feet as quickly as she could and looked around to be sure no one had seen. Assured that no one was in sight, she brushed herself off.

She noticed some little spots of blood on her arms and plenty of dirt on her clothes. She picked the pebbles off that were indented into her palms and forearms. She wiped her face with the back of her hand. She felt more gravel embedded into her cheeks and forehead. She must really look a mess. How could she go through the village looking like this?

She took her veil and shook out anything that might have stuck to it and replaced it over her face, back where it belonged. Then she put her shawl over her head loosely and limped with her head down. Maybe no one would notice her.

When she had entered the house her mother looked at her shocked and rushed to her side. "Mary Elizabeth, are you all right? Where have you been so early?"

"I am fine. I awoke and could not sleep, so I got dressed and walked to the rock where Joseph is building his and Mary's house. I sat there until the sun came up and, as I was climbing down off the rock, I slipped on some loose rocks and fell. I am dirty and embarrassed, but other than that, I am fine."

Theresa, still worried, said, "Go change into some clean clothes and clean up before your father sees you."

Dutifully, Mary Elizabeth walked quietly to her bedroom where Sarah was sleeping. She changed her clothes and looked into the mirror that John had given her. She found some more small pebbles embedded in her cheek. She picked them out and then washed her hands and face carefully making sure that she did not scrub too hard and make her face bleed again where the pebbles had been.

Sufficiently clean, Mary Elizabeth awakened her sister, "Sarah, Mama has the meal ready. We are just waiting for you."

"Where did you go in the middle of the night, Mary Elizabeth?" Sarah asked impatiently.

"Nowhere important, I just went for a walk."

"What are those red spots on your face? Are you ill? Maybe we should tell Mama. You should probably stay home today. You do not look well at all", Sarah commented.

"I am just fine. Maybe it is just a little blemish. I am sure that tomorrow my face will look better."

ॐ∘ॐ

"Mary, can we go to your room and talk. I have had another dream."

The girls both knew they could not go to the rock because Joseph might be there.

"Come with me.

"Mother, we are going to my room to talk. If you need me, let me know", Mary called.

The girls went behind the curtain. Mary peeked out to make sure they were alone and could not be heard.

"Go ahead, Mary Elizabeth. What happened?" Mary whispered.

"Well, this time the person was a man. He was handsome. Wonderfully dark hair to about his shoulders, a ruddy complexion, piercing eyes, robes of the purest white, and sandals on his feet.

"At first he was sitting on a hill with his legs crossed talking to a large group of people. There must have been a thousand or more. There were men, women and children all listening intently to what he was saying.

"Then the scene changed. The weather was stormy. It was dark with lightening all around. There was a lake or a sea. I could not tell which, but I knew it was a lot of water. The waves were breaking over the sides of a ship. My heart was racing because it looked as if the ship were going to sink. He stood and bid the water to be calm and it was so.

"The scene changed again. Again there was a lot of water but this time there was no storm. And the strangest thing, he was walking on the water. Everything was so peaceful. One of the men in the ship tried to walk on the water with the first man but he soon started to sink. The man in the white robe caught the other man by the arm and helped him to the ship.

Again, a different scene appeared. He was walking throughout the countryside healing the sick. He healed the blind, the dumb, the lame, the deaf, even lepers; anyone who was not whole. He commanded evil spirits to leave people who were afflicted. He was amazing. I wanted to be with him and watch his miracles.

"Then I awoke. That was the end of the dream."

Mary was quiet for a while. She seemed to be deep in thought. She arose and walked to the window and stared at nothing.

Then she said in a voice that was so soft that Mary Elizabeth could hardly hear her, "You are so favored of the Lord. Do you understand what is going on?"

Mary Elizabeth sat pondering what Mary had just said and then answered, "I think so. I think I am looking at the life of someone extremely important."

"Yes, I still think it is the Savior", Mary said truthfully.

"But I thought the Savior was supposed to come into the world on a white charger to save us all from the oppression of Rome?" Mary Elizabeth responded.

"Yes, but who else could it be?" Mary asked.

"I really do not have any idea. You said he was to be born in Bethlehem. How could he be born in Bethlehem and still come into the world on a white charger to fight for our freedom?" Mary Elizabeth asked logically.

"This is definitely a puzzle. I cannot figure it out.

"You are right, I did say both things. He should be born in Bethlehem and come on a white charger, also how can he be a Nazarene and be born in Bethlehem? Now I am as confused as you are", Mary admitted.

"Maybe he will be born in Bethlehem, be raised in Nazareth and when he is grown appear on a white charger to save the world" Mary Elizabeth said trying to prove her point by logistics.

৵৵৶

The next few months the girls spent making things for their new homes-to-be. They knew they must be prepared for their new dwellings. They wanted them to be pretty as well as homey and functional.

With the cloth bought from the caravan, the task looked easy. However, they found out that sewing was not as easy as their mothers had made it look. Praise be to Jehovah that they each had mothers that could help them when things did not turn out the way they thought they should.

They were not able to spend much time with each other. They were busy with their mothers. The mothers knew what they would need to begin married life.

This was the first marriage of any of Abraham and Theresa's children, but Jacob and Naomi's Mary Saphronia had been married a few years earlier. So of course, Naomi knew what the girls needed. The mothers were ambitiously engaged in making sure that the girls knew how to do everything that a good wife should. Sometimes they may have been a little too ambitious.

The mothers seemed to be working with reserved energy they had been saving up for just such an occasion. The girls could hardly keep up with them. Even Naomi seemed to muster up energy she had not displayed in many years.

Once in a while the girls would get together to compare notes. Of course the mothers did the same.

The men were spending their spare time making houses for them and their new wives to live in. They would no longer be living with their parents behind the bakery or carpenter's shop.

The homes would be small to begin with, but there would be room to expand when the children started coming along.

When Joseph had mentioned he would like to build his and Mary's house by the girl's favorite rock, the girls got together to talk and decided it would be wonderful. Then the rock would always belong to at least one of them. Mary Elizabeth felt confident that they would both still sit upon the top of the rock when they needed to. There was no other place on earth where they would feel comfortable enough to talk about secret and sacred things.

Consequently, they did not have much time to see the men. However, every so often the girls would go to the building sites and peek at the progress being made. They usually went when the men would not be working so they could look without being disturbed and without disturbing the men.

They wandered through the houses planning what items would go in which places. They still did not have much, but they felt they each had some great ideas.

The girls had often wondered why the marriages took place a year after the Betrothal. Now they were sure they understood. With all of the preparations to be made, houses and household items, it would probably take a year to accomplish it all.

❧◦❧

"Mary." The girl was sound asleep.

"Mary." The voice was soft and soothing.

She was sleeping so soundly that she still did not hear it.

A little louder this time, "Mary, arise".

Now she awoke, but being confused and seeing nothing, Mary turned over and tried to go back to sleep.

"Mary, awake and arise." The voice was a little sterner.

The maiden was so startled that she jumped out of bed.

Had she actually heard something or was it all a dream. She was wide awake but there was no one else in the room. She looked around and noticed a beam of light coming through her window. It was much brighter than she had ever seen. It could not be the moon. The light was much too bright. Besides, the direction that her room faced, the moon never came in her window. What was going on?

Finally, she heard a voice; a very lovely, soft voice. "Mary, you are a chosen vessel unto the Lord." The voice was so faint that she could not really hear where it was coming from.

She walked to the window and was bathed in the resplendent rays. The room suddenly filled with light brighter than noonday.

She was quivering with fear. The level of her anxiety was so high that she could feel her face flush. "Lord, what do you mean?"

"You have been chosen to bring My Son into the world", the voice said.

Not wanting to argue, but being totally confused she asked, "How can this be? I have not been with a man."

"You have been chosen because of your purity before me. You were chosen before the world was. I knew then that you would be the one."

"But, Lord, everyone thinks that Mary Elizabeth is the 'Chosen One'. She has been having dreams."

"Yes, she has been having dreams. Mary Elizabeth will always be a dreamer as long as she stays clean before me", the voice said. She also is pure before me and she is a Prophetess to her people. However, they are a stiff-necked people and will not believe her prophesying.

Woe unto them. But it is you who is the 'Chosen One'."

"How will this be done, Lord?"

"The Holy Ghost will come upon you this night and you will conceive and be with child, My Child, Mine Only Begotten Son, The Holy One of Israel."

"But Father, I am betrothed to Joseph. If he knows that I am with child and it is not his, he will leave me to be stoned by the people of the village. I will be called an adulteress", Mary almost screamed in panic.

"When I leave you, I will go to Joseph to tell him of my wondrous news. You are to tell no one of the baby which you will be carrying in your womb.

"You will be married right away and will not be stoned. You must not go unto Joseph in his bed until after the time of your purification. Remember that the child which you will carry in your womb is Holy. You are my vessel. Be calm and know that I am God."

All Mary could say was, "Thy will be done".

The light gathered in one place and then it was gone just as quickly as it had appeared.

When Mary realized that the light was gone, she found herself lying on her bed.

[How could all this be? Was I dreaming or did this really happen?]

She touched her abdomen in a circular motion with the palm of her hand.

[Am I carrying the Son of God? Is he now within my womb?

I must see Joseph, I long to see Joseph. Will he understand? Will he still love me? What will I do if he does not?]

Soon, she was; once again fast asleep.

છ∞ન્ડ

Joseph could not sleep. He had awoken abruptly and could not return to his wonderfully, needful sleep. He was so tired because his work at the carpenter's shop was exhausting enough without working on the house in his spare time. What spare time? It seemed he was wearing himself out. How much longer could he keep up this pace?

He decided this would be a good time to finish the cradle he was making for a man in Sappora. It was still dark; too dark to work on his and Mary's house.

As he entered the shop, he groped in the dark for the lantern.

Finding it, he turned it up along with the others so he would have enough light to work by.

There, [that should suffice]

As he was chiseling the engraving on the top of the cradle, he thought he heard something. It was a soft noise. Maybe a mouse was scampering across the room.

Then he heard it again, only this time it was a voice. He looked out the window to see if someone were outside. The moon shone brightly, so he could see clearly. No, not a soul was in sight.

"Joseph…Joseph listen to what I have to say."

Joseph turned toward the window and a pillar of light was coming through. The light had not been there before. He had just come from the window. What could make a light this bright. He went to the door and looked out. There was nothing out there. "Joseph, listen to what I have to say."

"I am listening, Lord." Joseph was trembling as he looked into the light. Who was there?

The light then filled the room as it had with Mary. Nothing else could be seen because of the brightness.

"Mary is with child. And you will call his name Jesus."

Joseph dropped the tool that was in his hand. It fell to the floor with a thud. He grabbed at his hair with both hands and yanked on both sides of his head.

He gained a minute amount of composure and then cried aloud in anguish, "This cannot be." And then very calmly and carefully, "Not so, Lord, I have not lain with her", he said confidently.

"It is so, Joseph. Mary is with child, My Child."

"But Lord, I do not understand. How can she be with child if no man has lain with her? What am I to do? We are betrothed, I love her."

He then sat down on a stool nearby, put his feet on the highest rung, put his elbows on his knees and squeezed his temples as tightly as he could and continued, "We can no longer be married. This will bring disgrace to both of our families. I must stand back and watch her be stoned."

"No, my son, it is all right. Mary carries mine only Begotten, conceived by the Holy Ghost. It is my will.

"What should I do, Lord?"

"Marry her right away and all will be well with you and her. Do not tell anyone of this event. And remember my words, you must not lay with her until after the time of her purification. The child within her womb is holy and precious in my sight."

"Yes, Lord, thy will be done." And he bowed on one knee in humble submission.

෨∘෨

Miracles of Jesus: New Testament KJV
Teaching: Matt. 4:17, 5, 6 and7
Healing: Matt. 4:23, 8:5-10, 14 and 15, 12:10-13. Mark 1:34. Many others
Leper: Matt. 8:2and3. Mark 1:40-43
Evil Spirits: Matt. 8:16, 8:28-33
Calmed the Sea: Matt. 8:23-26. Mark 4:37-40
Walked on Water: Matt. 14:22-33
Healed the Blind: Matt. 9:27-30, Mark 8:22-26, Mark 10:46-52
Healed the Deaf: Mark 7:32-34
Healed the Dumb: Mark 9:18
Mary and Joseph visited by the angel: Matt. 1:19-25
I took quite a bit of literary license in telling the story of Mary's conception and the reactions of both Mary and Joseph. Little is told in the New Testament about the event, so I added my ideas as to how these events might have occurred to try to make the story more interesting and flow better.

CHAPTER
SIX

"Mary, I had to see you." Joseph had walked to Mary's house at first light. He asked her to walk with him to the house he was building by the rock.

"But we must be properly chaperoned. I will ask Sarah to accompany us. She can walk a suitable distance behind us", Mary replied.

They walked slowly to the nearly completed house. The outside was finished. All he had to do was finish the interior and move their belongings in. They entered the house with Joseph going first so that he could be sure there was nothing on the floor that Mary could get hurt on. After looking around carefully, he motioned for Mary and Sarah to enter.

Sarah continued to stay back as far as she could in the small house. Then she decided she could probably stay outside as long as she kept the two lovebirds in sight.

Joseph was nervous and felt very defenseless. How was he supposed to say what was in his heart?

Mary looked surprised. She had wanted to talk to him, too. She had not decided how to tell him what had happened during the night. She tried to compose herself. She would tell him right out. If he did not want to marry her, she would understand and go away to have this child by herself in some far distant land.

Or, maybe, she could stay with her cousin Elisabeth and her husband Zacharias. They would take good care of her.

Before she could say anything, Joseph put his finger on her lips so she would not speak. "I had a visitor last night. He told me all that has happened to you."

They spoke softly so Sarah would not hear.

Mary started to cry. It could not be helped. Joseph knew the truth. What was he going to do? Would he feel shame?

Sarah, seeing Mary crying, came in and said, "Mary, are you alright?"

"Yes, Sarah, these are tears of relief. I am fine, please stay outside."

Joseph wiped the tears from her cheeks with his calloused hands. He loved her so much and she was so vulnerable. She was so wonderful. His Mary, the mother of the Holy One. He was struck with awe just looking at her and being in her presence. How had he fallen in love with such a special creature? She was perfect and he was just a humble carpenter.

"It will be all right, Mary. We will be married tomorrow night if that is all right with you."

"Yes." She lowered her eyes and looked at the floor. How had she been so fortunate as to have fallen in love with such a perfect man?

Joseph lifted her chin with his finger and kissed her softly on her tear stained lips and they melted unashamedly into one another's arms.

Sarah looked on, not knowing what it was all about, but she said nothing.

❧

The girls had not seen much of each other the past couple of weeks.

Mary Elizabeth felt that it had been far too long since she had seen her best friend except on the Sabbath in the Synagogue, so she told her mother that she needed a day off from making her home beautification projects. It was time to go see Mary.

She waited until mid-morning so, hopefully, Mary would be done with the normal daily tasks that had to be completed each day except on the Sabbath.

As she walked to Mary's house, she noticed the girl sitting outside on a rock near the road. This rock was not nearly as large as one the two girls always went to. It was only big enough for one person to sit on and then her feet touched the ground. Their special rock had to be climbed and no one's feet would come close to touching the ground.

Mary looked desolate, like she was in a world that only she was able to enter. She did not even see Mary Elizabeth coming.

"What is wrong, Mary? Has something happened?"

"Yes, Joseph and I are getting married right away. He says he cannot be without me any longer and I feel the same way", Mary said trying to sound convincing.

"I do not believe this. How can this be happening? I thought we were going to have a double wedding. What happened to all of our plans? Our wedding is only a couple of months away. I would think the two of you could wait that long."

"It happened all of a sudden. Joseph came to the house and talked with my father and said he did not want to wait."

Mary Elizabeth looked thoughtfully for a moment and then said, "What did your father say?"

Mary was so quiet that it scared Mary Elizabeth. She had never seen her friend so sullen. What had happened to make their plans change so quickly? Something was not right here. It just did not make sense.

Mary looked at her playmate of old, "He said he would talk to me and then make a decision. We talked a few minutes and decided that this was what we both really wanted.

"Besides, like you said, the wedding would be in a couple of months, anyway. We will be married tomorrow night.

"With the help of my mother, I have made just about everything needed to provide for our home. The house is almost finished. The last things to do are inside and we can live in it while the finishing touches are added. We will not have much furniture for a while, but Joseph can make what we need a little at a time."

The statement about the wedding finally hit Mary Elizabeth, "Tomorrow night? How are you going to do this?" she said in total shock.

"Mother and Father will work very hard to accomplish it. It will not be easy. They were quite upset when the decision was first made, but they have been wonderful about the whole thing. Of course, not many of our relatives will be there. But the important thing is that all of our friends will be. They are the most important ones to us."

Mary Elizabeth could not hide her disappointment. "When were you going to tell me? Would you have had the wedding and then told me when it was all over?"

Mary wrapped her arms tightly around her friend and laid her head on Mary Elizabeth's shoulder. When they came apart, Mary Elizabeth could see that tears were beginning to form in the corner of each of Mary's eyes. Through the blur she said, "I was just on my way over to see you. You know I would not leave you out. You will always be my best friend.

"The kind of friendship we have is unusual. I do not think anyone could be closer than we are.

"Please forgive me for not saying anything sooner. Things have been so hectic around here that I have not had time to think straight."

"Mary, is something wrong? I have never seen you this way before. I do not understand your mood. Are you not happy about the marriage? I would think you would be a lot more excited."

"I guess I am still in a state of shock. I am not fully used to the idea that tomorrow I will be a married woman. I am a little scared, too. I know I love him and that I am ready; I just did not expect the wedding to be this soon", Mary confessed.

By this time both of the girls were crying. They looked at each other and began laughing through the tears. They threw their arms around each other again and hugged so tightly that their backs felt like they would break.

"I am really happy for both of you", Mary Elizabeth said. "I am just disappointed that our wedding plans have changed, especially when it took so much to convince our Mothers to go along with it."
"I feel bad about that, too, but this is what we want.

"Please give us your blessing and say that you will be there. I do not think I would be happy in my marriage if you were not at the wedding."

"Please do not worry. I would not miss it for the world."

❧◦❧

Joseph walked to the bakery. John looked surprised when Joseph entered.

"Good morning, Joseph. What brings you out so early?" Benjamin asked.

"I wanted to talk to John", Joseph stated without any emotion in his voice.

"Come with me, Joseph. We can talk in the back room", John returned. With that, they retreated and closed the curtain behind them. "I came to invite you to my wedding tomorrow night", Joseph said with a big grin on his face.

John looked at him in disbelief. He could not give credence to what he was hearing. "What happened, is Mary with child?"

John meant that as a joke, but it came out very serious. If Mary was with child and they did not marry right away she would be stoned. But he knew in his heart that she was a virgin. He knew that Joseph would not disgrace his beloved. There had to be another explanation.

"Actually, I cannot bear to wait any longer. I love her so much that I want to be with her now… Maybe we *can* have a child before too long."

Joseph knew he had not told the whole truth, but a secret like his and Mary's was not to be made public. Besides, who would believe it, anyway? "You will come, of course."

"Absolutely, we will all be at your wedding."

The two men embraced and then told Benjamin the good news. Then Joseph hurried out the door.

[Whew, that is over. John was told and no one was the wiser. That was a close one.

Mary's time will be in just nine months and then she will be totally mine.]

❧◦❧

This is the day. The canopy is set up. Joseph and Mary are ready to be married.

Mary Elizabeth is happy and sad at the same time. She was happy for the loving couple, but she is sad that she has to wait for two months before she can get married.

☙❧

It is time for the marriage ceremony to begin. Joseph has his white gown over his clothes and Mary has her white gown on and the veil draped across her face.

They both fasted today. That was a decision they made together. They felt that the spirit would be stronger if they did. It is meant to be a spiritual experience and that is the way they want it.

All the guests are seated.

The Rabbi stands and addresses the couple, "Marriage is the ideal state. The Talmud reads 'He who has no wife is not a proper man.'

"The family has always been the strength of Judaism. Indeed, Judaism may be able to survive with the Synagogue, but the Synagogue cannot survive without the family.

"The Jewish wedding sets the tone for your future Jewish life." He paused and looked lovingly at the Bride and Groom before continuing. "The Jewish family is not a partnership, it is a merger of two individuals, with two minds and personalities and characteristics and genes. In other words, the merger will not be easy to achieve but when the family is established it is at least twice as strong as before the wedding.

"When you stand and repeat the ritual phrases, you must remember that you have taken a step closer to holiness. You have become consecrated to each other. Two souls become fused into one family, an everlasting entity, destined to share each other's future."

Mary and Joseph looked at one another and the bride blushed.

"This ceremony is leading to the creation of a home that will become a small sanctuary."

Before the ring ceremony the Rabbi leads the bride and groom in reciting two blessings and a sip of wine.

At this time Joseph placed the ring on Mary's right forefinger, and said in Hebrew, "You are consecrated unto me with this ring according to the laws of Moses and Israel".

The couple then sipped some more wine and Joseph took the empty glass and stomped on it, breaking it as a remembrance of the Temple that was destroyed in Jerusalem at the time of the capture of Jerusalem by Nebuchadnezzar.

Then the audience stood up and cheered as Joseph and Mary, now legally married, embraced and kissed.

The ceremony was over. Everyone began hugging and kissing the happy couple. They were now one with Jehovah.

The party began. Singing and dancing could be heard everywhere in the village. There was plenty of food and abundance of only the finest wine.

Jacob and Naomi had outdone themselves and no one could figure out how they had done it.

Mary Elizabeth sat by John during the wedding and could be seen holding hands. They ate together and danced together. She hated it when he had to go home. She wished that the night would last forever, well, at least until their own wedding. She even wished that this had been their wedding, too. But there was no way that they were anywhere near ready for their wedding. She did not have any idea how Joseph and Mary had pulled it off. It was a perfectly wonderful occasion.

The wedding had strengthened John's love for Mary Elizabeth. He could only dream of their wedding day and his first night with his new bride.

Mary Elizabeth fell into a deep sleep when she got home. She was so tired she thought she might sleep away the next two months and wished she could. She ached from sitting on the hard ground and all the dancing, but it was worth it. Her heart ached for love of John. She had had a wonderful time. Yes, it was worth it...

Joseph took Mary to their new home in the wee hours of the morning and retired.

"Joseph, this is not going to be easy for either of us. It is hard to have to wait to consummate our marriage", Mary said apologetically.

❧

Mary Elizabeth was having a marvelous dream about her and John's wedding. She could see the canopy, her and John in their wedding attire and the guests seated on the floor. Everything looked perfect. She awoke. It was still dark outside. She would try to go back to sleep and get back into her amazing dream.

[I wish I could dream about my wedding forever, at least until the real thing.]

Quickly, she was sleeping again, but instead of dreaming about her wedding, it was a horrifying nightmare. She was unable to awaken herself. She knew that it was just a dream however, it was as real as if she were standing there a part of the whole terrible scene.

When she finally did awake it was already sun-up. Just as she was stretching, her mother came into the room to wake the girls. "I have started breakfast. Please come and help."

Sarah remarked, "Mary Elizabeth, what is wrong? You have tears running down your face and your eyes are all red and puffy."

"I just had a bad dream. I guess I ate too much last night", was Mary Elizabeth's excuse.

Both girls were up and dressed. They washed their hands and faces and brushed their hair.

The older sister made sure to pat her eyes with the cool water to reduce the swelling.

Mary Elizabeth was unusually quiet. Who could she talk to now? It would be inappropriate for her to go to Mary's house. Joseph would be there. He would not go to the shop for at least a month. He needed to be home and get to "know" his wife. That is the way it is done.

Maybe her mama would listen. Although, she was the one who started the rumor about her being the mother of the Messiah.

Who could she talk to? Maybe Mary would go to the well for water. That would not work. Probably Joseph would go with her.

John would be the next alternative. Would he think she was hallucinating? Would he make light of the dream? Would he have time or be willing to listen to her? There was only one way to find out. When her chores were done she would go to the bakery.

It was still quite early when she arrived at the bakery. John was behind the table arranging the bread in an orderly manner.

When he saw Mary Elizabeth enter, you could see the love on his face and the twinkle in his eyes that he had inherited from his father.

Benjamin was just coming from the back room with a heavy tray full of "fresh-out-of-the-oven" delicacies. Everything smelled sensational today.

Mary Elizabeth's stomach was not so jittery anymore; at least not until the wedding day gets nearer.

"Mary Elizabeth, how wonderful that you should drop in", Benjamin stated in earnest. "We are always glad to see you. How is your mother?" He was surprised to see her without a chaperone. He would have to serve as the chaperone while they were together in the bakery.

"Mother is fine. She is very busy these days with the wedding so close."

"Ahhh", was the only remark.

"I would like to talk with John alone, if I may."

"Of course, but without a chaperone?" Benjamin said, as he looked warily at her, knowing that she should not be alone with him.

"It is very important. We will stay where we will be seen. We will not be entirely alone.

"John, could we go for a walk? I have something very serious to talk to you about and I would rather we not be disturbed."

John, wondering what he had done wrong, followed her out the door.

They walked to a large Cyprus tree near the edge of town, being sure not to touch each other. Being unchaperoned was bad enough, but any public display of affection was unthinkable.

When they arrived at the tree they sat in the shade. Mary Elizabeth took off her sandals and tucked her knees up under her clothes and wrapped her arms around her legs to be more comfortable.

John just sat stiff and looked as though if a strong gust of wind should blow by, he would tip over.

As Mary Elizabeth became comfortable, she began to speak from the heart. "John, I have had a dream. I hope you do not mind my telling it to you. Now that Mary and Joseph are married, I cannot go to her because they are using this time to become better acquainted."

"Speak on", John said with some apprehension.

Mary Elizabeth did not want to stumble over her words, so she took her time.

"In my dream the sun was gone, but I could tell that it was still day. There was thunder and lightning all around, the earth was quaking and I saw a hill." She paused and looked around to see if anyone was close by. Then she continued, "On the hill there were three crosses. There were three men hanging on the crosses. Somehow I knew that the one in the middle was someone extremely important. The ones on either side were thieves. Then she paused again, this time to take a big breath of air before going on. "I do not know how I knew this, but it was made known to me.

"The one in the middle had something on his head that looked like a crown, but it seemed to have thorns on it because there were small drops of blood at the spots where the thorns pierced his brow. There was also blood where the nails were in his hands, wrists and feet.

He wore nothing but a piece of cloth draped about his loins. At the top of the cross it read, 'King of the Jews'.

"There were people who were watching, crying. Others were mocking him.

"When it was made known to me that he was dead, it started to rain. And it rained hard. I felt like the angels in Heaven were crying too because of the horrifying sight. I remember that I was weeping, too, but that no one could tell because it was raining so hard that my face was drenched.

"Two Roman soldiers came and touched the man in the middle with a sword. The man did not move. Then one of the soldiers thrust his sword into the side of the man and water gushed out.

"I could not bear to watch. I hid my face and sobbed into my hands.

"That was all. When I awoke my bed and my face were soaked."

John just looked at Mary Elizabeth. He was so awe stricken that he did not know what to say. Then finally he said, "We have been taught that the Messiah will come and that he will be hung on a tree between two malefactors. Maybe it is He." His voice was choked. The words did not want to come out. But finally he said so softly she could hardly hear him, "Maybe…it…is…He." His head was bent low in a very reverent manner.

"John, it was so astonishing to me because I had never seen such a thing before. I have heard of it, but something about it really bothered me. I cannot explain it. Maybe I never will be able to.

"Please do not think ill of me. I love you and could not bear it if you thought I was mad.

"Maybe it was just a nightmare. Maybe it does not mean anything." She put both of her hands over her face and cried.

John stood up and gently pulled his beloved up also.

"Mary Elizabeth, please look at me."

She looked up at his magnificent face and into his loving eyes. How could anyone be sad around him?

"Remember, you can always come to me. I may not have all the answers, but I am here for you. I will always listen to whatever you have to say."

John put both of his arms around his espoused and pulled her into him with no resistance. She buried her head in his chest and wept uncontrollably.

∂∘∝

The wedding ceremony was taken from the Torah and "Under the Wedding Canopy: Love & Marriage in Judaism" by David C. and Ester R. Gross p.28

Mary Elizabeth's dream was taken from the KJV of the bible Matt. 27:37-38 and 51, Mark 15:25-27, Luke 23:33, John 19:17-20 and 34

CHAPTER
SEVEN

Mary and Joseph were trying to get their lives somewhat back to some kind of normalcy. Joseph was back at the carpentry shop during the day and at home in the evening.

Mary took care of her house and was able to see Mary Elizabeth quite often. The latter was still busy preparing things for her new home, which was coming along nicely.

John was not building their house near Mary and Joseph, but Mary Elizabeth was sure that they would visit each other often. It was now only a few weeks until their wedding. The bride and groom were both getting nervous and anxious; nervous, because the time was getting so close and anxious because the time seemed to be dragging. They could see how happy Mary and Joseph were and they wanted that same happiness.

Mary Elizabeth told Mary of her latest dream. Mary listened and agreed with John's explanation. And she said she was sorry that she could not have been there for Mary Elizabeth when she was needed.

One day, when least expected, Mary announced, "I am with child".

Mary Elizabeth was shocked, "Are you sure? It is awfully soon. Maybe you missed because of the excitement of being newly married."

"No, I am sure. I can feel the baby growing in my womb", Mary gestured as she swept her hand in a circular motion over her abdomen. "I feel like fainting every time I smell food cooking or some other odors I am unaccustomed to."

"It sure sounds like that is the problem. Are you sure it might not be the ague?" Mary Elizabeth asked.

"I am very sure.

"Joseph is elated. I was on my way over to tell my parents the good news. Do you want to come along?" Mary inquired.

"No, you go ahead. I will meet up with you later."

Things were different. Her best friend was married. Mary is anticipating the arrival of a child in a few months. Joseph was now her best friend. How could anything ever be the same again?

The next few weeks rushed by quickly. Mary Elizabeth had been busy putting finishing touches on her household items. John had been working on the house as much as possible and it looked great.

Joseph finished the inside of his and Mary's house. It was all that she had hoped for.

Mary's baby was growing inside of her. If she held her clothes tight against her, she could feel a slight bump. It was real. She was really going to give birth to the Son of God. She could not believe that she had been married for two months and she was still a virgin. This was not the way it was supposed to be in marriages, but when you have a holy child within your body, it cannot be otherwise. The baby must not be defiled.

☙❧

John and Mary Elizabeth were married and living in their new home. Life was good.

(There were a lot of rumors going around about Joseph and Mary. People had heard that she was going to have a baby. Most said that it was too soon. They were accusing her of the most sinful accusations. That *must* be the reason that she and Joseph had been married so soon.

Joseph could not be blamed. After all, he was a man and his feelings were hard to keep within him. It was a difficult thing not to take his betrothed before the wedding. Being betrothed was almost like being married, except it did not afford the wedding night customs.

Mary was another matter. After all, it was her place to keep her virginity intact until after the marriage ceremony.)

Mary walked to Mary Elizabeth's house. Her condition was getting more and more obvious. She was now three months into her inception.

"Mary Elizabeth, are you home?" called the cheerful voice.

Mary Elizabeth went to the door and greeted her friend with a big hug. "Come in and sit. I will get you a cool cup of water."

"Thank you. I have some news", Mary said.

"I hope it is good. I could use some good news", the homeowner stated.

"Well, I think it is. My cousin Elisabeth, who lives near Jerusalem, is close to delivering her child.

"Actually, she is my mother's cousin, but I love her dearly. I have not seen her since I was a young girl. She was not able to attend the wedding because there was no time to notify her. I am sure she would have come otherwise.

"She has never had a child and she should be far past bearing age. We just learned that she is six months into her inception. I am going to see her and stay awhile. She needs some help. She will probably have a difficult time because of her age. I am really excited", Mary finished.

"What about Joseph, are you leaving him at home?" Mary Elizabeth asked as she handed her friend the cool refreshment.

"Well, it was his idea. He has extra work to do at the shop because of the time taken after our wedding. Even though, he should have taken more time off, his father became busy with orders and was not able to keep up, even with the help of the other sons.

"This will give him more time to finish what he has started.

Besides, he said he thought it would be good for me to get away for a while. It has been especially difficult with all of the gossip. It will give me something else to think about."

"You cannot leave. I do not know what I will do without you." "Mary Elizabeth, stop that. You will do just fine. You have your wonderful husband. You probably won't even miss me.

"Well, I must go and put a few things together in a bag. A man that my father knows from Cana will be picking me up in the morning. He has a wagon and needs to go to Jerusalem for some supplies", Mary explained as she returned her cup to the table.

"You are going alone with a man all the way to Jerusalem?" It was evident that Mary Elizabeth was concerned for the welfare of her friend.

"No, I would never do that. His wife and three children are going, too. I will have plenty of company."

"How long do you think it will take?" Mary Elizabeth questioned.

"I am not sure; a lot depends on the weather and road conditions, hopefully, not more than a week.

"Are you sure it will be all right for the baby? You do not want to take any unnecessary chances", Mary Elizabeth added trying to encourage her to change her mind.

"It is all set. I am leaving in the morning."

Mary spread her arms apart and invited Mary Elizabeth to enter and then they hugged tightly.

"I am going to miss you. I do not know what I will do while you are gone", Mary Elizabeth said as tears were forming in her eyes. "How long will you be gone?"

"Probably until Elisabeth has her baby. I might stay a little longer and help her get back on her feet. Having a baby is quite an ordeal for any woman, but with Elisabeth's age it could be complicated."

The girls hugged again. Then Mary exited out the door. "Thank you for the water. It was just what I needed."

When John came home for the mid-day meal it was very clear that his wife had been crying.

He took her into his arms in a long embrace and then finally asked, "What is wrong, My Love?"

"Mary is leaving for Jerusalem in the morning and will be gone for about three months."

"Yes, I know. I saw Joseph this morning. He told me that she should get away for a while", John said while stroking her long hair, trying to soothe her. "Please do not be upset. It worries me when you are sad.

"You have much to do around here. You will see…time will pass by quickly. It will be no time at all until she will be back."

"I hope so", Mary Elizabeth confided. "We have been together all of our lives. The only time we have been separated was after each of our weddings. I will just feel so alone."

"That hurts. You know I am here. You will always have me. I am not going anywhere", John voiced.

Mary Elizabeth reached up and put both of her hands on her husbands' cheeks and looking into his gray-blue eyes said, "You are so wonderful. I would never want to hurt you.

"Please understand, I know you are here for me and I could never love anyone as much as I love you. You are my heart, my soul, my whole being. It is just hard for me to let go of Mary. We have been close all of our lives. This idea of being married is new to me. I sometimes forget that there is someone more important to me now. Please forgive me for being such a fool. I will be all right now. Talking to you was just what I needed to do. Thank you."

With that, she pulled him down to her level and kissed him hard on the lips and clung to him a long time with her arms securely fastened around his neck.

૭ન્ટ્ડ

Jacob, Lois, Mordecai, Amos and Judah were at the well at sun-up with the wagon and two mules for pulling. Mary was waiting for them; Joseph beside her.

"Are you sure you want to go?" Joseph questioned his wife. "You can still back out. I am sure Elisabeth could find someone else to help."

"I want to help. It will make me feel more worthwhile. I love taking care of you, but that does not keep me busy enough. Elisabeth will want to help me make clothes for the baby. I will not stay any longer than I am needed. I will miss you too much to overstay."

"You take care of yourself and that special little bundle you are carrying", He said as he put his hand firmly on her abdomen.

"I will. Please do not worry about me. I will be fine. While I am taking care of Elisabeth, I am sure she will want to mother and take care of me."

Joseph kissed Mary on the forehead and helped her up into the back of the wagon and then slipped her bag in alongside of her.

Within minutes she was on her way.

Joseph started walking sullenly back toward the carpentry shop. He looked up just in time to see Mary Elizabeth running toward him.

"I have come to see Mary off", she said as she was looking around for the wagon.

"She left just a few moments ago", Joseph reported.

Mary Elizabeth's anguish was readable on her face. "I missed her? How could I do that?

She fell to her knees and dropped her head into her open hands and sobbed.

[How could I be late? I wanted her to know that I support her decision to go to Jerusalem. Now she will not know until she gets back. How could I be late?]

Mordecai and Amos were sitting up front with Jacob. Lois and Judah were in the back with Mary.

"Are you with child?" Lois asked looking at Mary's face and then at the small swollen bump under her clothes.

"Yes, about three months", Mary said with pride.

Lois gave her a wary look and asked, "How long have you been married?"

Mary smiled, "A little over three months".

"You have a good man. He does not waste time.

"We were married almost two and a half years before I found out that I was in the motherly way", Lois said.

"We were fortunate. We wanted a baby right away and Jehovah made it happen", Mary smiled. [If Lois only knew, but then, no one must.]

"This one is my baby", Lois said as she smiled. "His name is Judah. He is not much of a baby anymore." Lois looked at her son with pride and then kissed him on top of his head.

"How old is he?" Mary asked inquisitively.

"Judah is four, Amos is twelve, and Mordecai is Sixteen. They are good boys." Anyone could see that she loved her family dearly.

The women talked for hours.

At about mid-day Jacob pulled the mules to a halt alongside of the road near a spring. The place was well-known as a good place to stop and rest the beasts for a while.

The women washed their hands and faces and then Lois washed Judah's in the spring water.

The other boys helped Jacob unhitch the mules and led them to the water for a hearty drink. They then washed up for the meal.

Lois reached into a large bag and produced a piece of dried meat and some fruit for them to eat. She tore the meat into pieces and gave them to the boys along with a piece of fruit. The children devoured the food quickly. They certainly had boy's appetites.

The mother made sure there was enough for Jacob and a little bit for herself. She offered some to Mary.

"You are too kind. Thank you, but I put enough food in my bag." Mary opened the bag beside her and brought out a piece of cheese and an apple that she had put there this morning. She smiled at Lois and thanked her again for her generosity. She ate it slowly to savor every mouthful. She was ravenous.

She missed Joseph already. Had it not been for Lois conversing with her, she probably would be crying.

Lois knew it would be hard for Mary, only having been married such a short amount of time, to be away from her bridegroom.

Secretly, she had always wanted a daughter. She never let Jacob know this because she was afraid of hurting his feelings. He loved his sons and was very proud of them as was Lois, but deep down, there was always that concealed yearning for a little girl she could raise and teach, cuddle and love. It would be fun to teach a little girl to cook and for her to learn womanly and motherly things that she was not able to teach her sons. Sons were able to learn from their father and he did a splendid job, too. But to have a girl…all she could do was dream and she did that often.

Mary was not her daughter but maybe somehow she could help make the trip more comfortable and divert her thinking away from Joseph for a while.

After the meal, Jacob climbed into the back of the wagon, laid his head on one of the bags and fell asleep.

The older boys found some small rocks and hurled them into the distance, competing for the longest throw, as brothers will. Of course, there was really no contest since Mordecai was older and much stronger.

Lois and Mary sat on the dirt with Judah and drew pictures. Pictures made in the dirt was great fun. If you did not like the picture, you could erase it with your hand and draw another. Judah enjoyed the game as did Mary. She was already learning how to have fun with a little boy. This was something she could savor with her own son.

Mary was starting to feel quite nauseous. It was time to take a nap. She must feel better; she had a long trip ahead of her. This was only the beginning. She had never experienced this side effect of being in the motherly way. She hoped it would not last long.

In about an hour Jacob was up and anxious to continue the trip. He and the boys hitched up the mules to the wagon making sure that the harnesses were tight. Everyone crawled up onto the wagon and they were on their way once again.

Mary was feeling somewhat better. She found that she could not sit in the wagon looking backward. Jacob insisted that Mary sit on the wagon seat with him. That *did* help…a little.

They drove most of the day. Just before sundown they decided to stop for the night so that they could get an early start in the morning.

The sky was rosy to the west. The sun would not be visible very long so they must hurry. There were some high rocks to the east and the sun made beautiful pictures of magenta, crimson and pink shapes against them.

Jacob got some blankets out of the wagon, folded them in half and put them on the ground beneath the wagon for Lois and him. He unhitched the mules and led them to water and then fed them fodder that he had brought with him in the back of the wagon.

While he was keeping busy with the mules, the boys were hunting for some kind of dead wood, which they could use for fire. It got cold at night and the fire would not only help keep them warm, but also would keep the wild animals away.

Lois reached into her bag once again and brought out some wonderful cheese, fruit, bread and some of the meat from the earlier meal.

Mary went to the river to get water. While she was there, she removed her sandals, waded into the creek, fully clothed and washed herself to get the days dust off as best she could and relaxed in the cool water. It felt good just to sit and enjoy the refreshing liquid moving about her tired body. She was homesick. She missed Joseph terribly. And now, it did not make her feel any better with the sickness she was having. She hoped this malady would not last too long.

The river they were near meandered lazily through the hills. It only ran fast during the spring thaw when the snow from the distant mountains emptied into it, otherwise it moved slowly as it was doing now. It was fun to watch the fish swimming along, which were going upstream, north to spawn. If Jacob and the boys could catch some they would have a delicious dinner. Mary would suggest it. She hated to get out of the refreshing water, but she should help get things ready for supper and make herself a bed for the night in the back of the wagon.

"Jacob, I was just down by the creek and I saw fish. I thought maybe you and the boys could catch some for dinner. I am really hungry", Mary admitted.

"What a wonderful idea. I can use some of the meat we have left for bait", Jacob returned. "Come boys, time to go fishing."

He and the boys caught the fish that was needed for the meal and they roasted them over the open fire. What a delicacy the roasted fish was and with the fruit and cheese, the dinner was perfect.

Everyone was satisfied and huddled next to the fire to keep warm.

The sun was hidden behind a distant hill by this time and the crickets were beginning to sing their favorite evening song. All was calm and peaceful.

The light on the distant rocks was no longer the Master's canvas of reddish hues. The campfire cast an eerie light now. A feeling of something foreboding filled Mary's breast. It was unexplainable. She decided she would go to sleep. Everyone else followed suit.

She had a hard time getting comfortable in the back of the wagon. She tossed and turned for a while and then finally settled down.

She had just dosed off when off in the distance she was startled when she heard the rumbling of horse's hooves.

She listened for a few seconds, but when the sound was getting closer she started to panic. "Jacob, do you hear that?" she yelled to the man under the wagon.

"Yes, Mary, I do. Try to stay calm. Hopefully, they will pass us by without knowing we are here", he said hurriedly as he jumped up and worked to throw dirt on the fire with the aid of Amos and Mordecai.

As luck would have it, they did not douse the fire in time.

Behind the rocks came five men on horseback like thunder. They were all dressed in black with their faces hidden except for their eyes.

Jacob stood in front of the women and children. He had nothing with which to protect himself or his family. All he could do was give them whatever they wanted and try not to show much fear. Mordecai and Amos stood right behind their father. They were all trying to protect the women. Men like these were noted for taking advantage of women, especially beautiful women such as these.

"Give us all of your food and money", the leader demanded in a harsh, gruff voice.

"Please, My Lord, take what you must but do not harm the women and children", Jacob begged.

"Ah yes, these are beautiful women. They could be a big comfort to us on these cold nights. Are they both yours?"

"Yes, Lord, they are my wives and the youngest is with child", Jacob stated with pride.

"Hmmm, with child", said the man as he looked Mary up and down. "You are a fortunate man. Where are you coming from?"

"Not too far from here. We are on an errand to Jerusalem", Jacob volunteered.

"What kind of errand?" asked the leader.

"I need to buy supplies for the mill I am building to grind grain for our villagers."

The leader looked the group of people over from head to foot and asked, "Are these your sons? I think we will take them with us. I am sure we can find some good use for them."

All of the men laughed in a way that made Mary's stomach turn.

"Lord, please do not take my sons, I need them in my business. They are my only help. As you can see, they are very young and still need their mother."

"The oldest one does not look very young. We could teach him many things that would be profitable to him and to us. The others will grow up quickly", the marauder stated as he was tormenting the travelers.

The men laughed a hearty laugh again. It was very unsettling.

"Your youngest wife would make a good wife for me. She is very beautiful. I would treat her very well. When the child is born we could sell it."

The man walked over to her and grabbed her chin and looked her over very carefully. The girl felt violated. She had a sinking feeling in the pit of her stomach. Suddenly the man let go of her and asked, "What is your name?"

"Mary, My Lord", the girl mumbled as she stood with her head bowed.

Ah, Mary", the ringleader said with tenderness.

"You have a long trip ahead of you. You had better get some sleep. Come men, we had better leave. There are more deplorable ones out there that will fill our needs", the commander shouted.

With that, the marauders were gone. As suddenly as they had appeared, they had taken their leave.

The sound of the galloping horses could be heard fading in the distance.

When all was quiet again, Mary asked, "Why did you tell them that I was your wife?"

"If I had not told them all that I did, they would have taken you and raped you and left you for dead somewhere out in the desert", Jacob said soberly.

Mary said nothing more. She was grateful to Jacob for his thoughtfulness. She lay down again in the rear of the wagon, closed her eyes and said a silent 'thank you' to Jehovah.

❧❦

Mary Elizabeth was tired. She had worked all day rearranging the living space in her new home. She decided to go to the bakery and have John stop by the carpenter's shop and ask Joseph to supper. That was the least she could do for her best friend's husband while she was gone.

She had heard some nasty talk when she was getting water at the well that morning.

("Where is your friend, Mary? Has she left her husband so soon? And her with child, tsk, tsk. Maybe it is not his child. Maybe it is the child of some caravan merchant. Perhaps, Joseph sent her away while he is getting a divorce. We would not blame him. After all, he was good enough to marry her and now she has taken leave to go who knows where.")

The gossip was more than she was able to handle. Who knew but what they were right.

No, not Mary, she was the most honest and honorable person Mary Elizabeth had ever known. To her, Mary was perfect.

The days would drag without Mary here to talk to. She was so used to having her companion close by. She could talk to Mary just about any time she wanted to and about anything. It was strange and lonely without her here.

Yes, she has John. He is her husband and is more than willing to be her best friend, but somehow, it was not the same. She loved him all the more for his effort.

Mary was her best friend, her sister, her confidant, her childhood cohort.

Mary Elizabeth put her shawl over her head and went out the door toward the bakery. It was already dark, so she hurried on.

The bakery was closed, but she could see John in the back still cleaning the floor. She rapped on the door.

"Go away. We are closed", was the reply.

"John, it is I, Mary Elizabeth."

"I am sorry, My Love, we have been so busy today that I have not had time to keep things clean like I should", John complained. "Come in and keep me company."

"I was just wondering if we could ask Joseph over for supper. Maybe it would cheer him up", Mary Elizabeth said.

We should stop on the way home. If he is still working, I will ask. He surely cannot spend all of his time in the shop", John remarked.

Mary Elizabeth bent over and kissed her husband on top of the head as he was picking something up off the floor.

☙❧

Again, I took the liberty of having Mary and Joseph get married before she went to see her cousin Elisabeth. In the King James Version of the New Testament, it states that she went to see Elisabeth, however, it does not state when the marriage took place. It is my opinion that they would have been married right after the angel visited Joseph. The bible doesn't say when the angel appeared to Joseph. I put in this sequence because to me it makes sense. I feel that a loving Heavenly Father would want them to be married right after the Holy Child was conceived to save embarrassment to the couple and their families.

CHAPTER
EIGHT

It was late in the afternoon when Jacob reined the mules in front of the home of Zacharias and Elisabeth.

Mary was excited to see her mother's cousin. She ran to the door just as Elisabeth opened it. They ran into each other's arms and embraced for what seemed like an eternity. They looked at each other and when they saw that both of them were crying for joy, they laughed.

Elisabeth looked at the family in the wagon and said, "Please come in. Let me get you some cool water and something to eat."

Jacob called from the transporter, "You are too kind. We just wanted to be sure Mary was all right. She is a wonderful girl."

Mary ran back to the wagon and hugged each member of the family individually. First she hugged Judah. She hoped her baby would be as sweet as he was. Somehow she knew he would. Although, he liked Mary he wriggled to get back into his mother's arms and clung to her with all of his might.

Amos was next to be on the receiving end of the embrace. He was embarrassed. Boys his age were like that. Mordecai surprisingly hugged her back tightly. He felt as though she were his younger sister he had never had.

Then she hugged Jacob, gave him a kiss on the cheek and whispered, "Thank you for everything". A tear could be seen in his eye, welling up in one corner.

Tears were streaming down both sides of Mary's face when she came to Lois. "You have been so good to me. I do not know how I would have survived the trip without you. You kept my mind occupied so that I did not dwell on missing my beloved Joseph."

"We must be on our way. Thank you for your kind offer", Jacob yelled to Elisabeth.

"No, thank you for bringing my cousin safely to me", Elisabeth retorted.

Mary and Elisabeth waved as the wagon drove off.

The elder woman put her arm around the younger woman's shoulders and led her into the house.

"Let me look at you." Elisabeth stood back so she could get a better view. All of a sudden she grabbed her abdomen and stiffened.

"Are you all right, My Cousin?" Mary inquired.

Elisabeth looked astonished. "I am fine. When I looked at you, my baby leaped inside of me". Then to Mary's astonishment she continued, "You are the 'Chosen One'. You are blessed among women, and blessed is the fruit of your womb. Why are we so honored that the mother of my Lord should come to visit us?"

Mary lowered her head in humility. "How did you know?" she said meekly.

"As soon as I looked at you the babe in my womb leaped for joy."

Elisabeth drew closer, took Mary by the hands and led her to the couch. When she sat, she patted the place beside her for Mary to sit. The girl sat softly next to Elisabeth. "This is a wonderful thing. My little Mary was chosen to be the mother of the Messiah. I can hardly believe it."

Mary arose and walked to the window and looked out and said, "My soul magnifies the Lord, and my spirit has rejoiced in God my Savior. For he has regarded the low estate of his handmaiden; for, behold, from this time forth all generations shall call me blessed. For he that is mighty has done to me great things; and holy is his name." As she continued she turned to face Elisabeth.

"And his mercy is on them that fear him from generation to generation. He has shown strength with his arm; he has scattered the proud in the imagination of their hearts. He has put down the mighty from their seats, and exalted them of low degree."

She lowered her head in humility.

"He has helped his servant Israel, in remembrance of his mercy; as he spoke to our fathers, to Abraham, and to his seed forever."

"I must rest", Elisabeth said as she lay down on the couch. "This has been an exhausting afternoon and I am not a young woman anymore.

"Does your mother know?" she said as an afterthought.

"No, we were instructed not to tell anyone."

Mary looked worried, "May I get you something; a cup of water; anything?"

"No, My Dear, I will be fine. Just let me rest awhile."

Zacharias came home from the temple a little late. When he walked into the house his eyes were wide with excitement as he saw Mary sitting on the floor near his wife.

"Look who is here", Elisabeth said as she addressed her husband.

He flung his arms open, gave the girl a big hug and rocked her back and forth.

When he let go, Mary backed off and looked alarmingly at the man. He had not said a word.

Elisabeth seeing the astonishment on Mary's face said, "I am sorry, I thought you knew".

"Knew what?" Mary returned.

"My husband had a vision in the temple as he was burning incense. In the vision he was told that I would bear a son and he is to be the forerunner of your child."

Zacharias looked at Mary in wonderment, thinking deeply about what he had just heard.

"It was an angel that appeared to him and said, "Thy wife Elisabeth shall bear thee a son, and thou shall call his name John.

"And thou shall have joy and gladness; and many shall rejoice at his birth.

"For he shall be great in the sight of the Lord, and shall drink neither wine nor strong drink; and he shall be filled with the Holy Ghost, even from his mother's womb.

"And many of the children of Israel shall he turn to the Lord their God.

"And he shall go before him in the spirit and power of Elias, to turn the hearts of the fathers to the children, and the disobedient to the wisdom of the just; to make ready a people prepared for the Lord."

And Zacharias said unto the angel, "Whereby shall I know this, for I am an old man, and my wife well stricken in years."

And the angel answering him said, "I am Gabriel, which stands in the presence of God; and am sent to speak unto thee, and to show thee these glad tidings."

Elisabeth continued with her story, "Zacharias disbelieved what the angel said because I was beyond bearing age and I have been barren all these years.

"And behold, you shall be dumb, and not able to speak, until the day that these things shall be performed, because you believed not my words, which shall be fulfilled in their season.' And it has been so."

"I am so sorry", Mary sympathized.

"Zacharias smiled and shrugged his shoulders. He was getting used to not talking. Besides, it kept him from having to explain to others about his experience.

That night they had a very informal and leisurely meal over which Mary told them of Joseph, the visit by the 'Angel of God', Joseph's visitation, the wedding and her house. It was so good just to be honest and to tell things that had been locked up inside of her for so long. She also told them of the trip and how Jacob had protected her from the thieves.

"Jacob is a good man", Elisabeth stated, "You were fortunate that it was his family you traveled with. Things could have gone another direction." She shuddered at the thought of what might have been.

"How long are you going to stay?" Elisabeth asked as she changed the subject.

"I thought I would stay until your baby is born. Joseph has a lot of work to catch up on. He will come for me sometime after 'The Festival of Lights'.

"I already miss him terribly, but I am glad that I had the chance to visit both of you", Mary explained as she held both of their hands over the table.

❧

"I hope you slept well", Elisabeth commented as Mary came from one of the back rooms.

"Very well, thank you."

"What would you like to do today?" the older woman asked.

"I really should visit my aunts while I am here", Mary replied, "but I will have plenty of time for that. We will do what you want to do."

"We shall do that then. I have no other plans. And besides, I have not seen the aunts since my inception. That should be a great surprise", Elisabeth giggled.

The women ate a relaxing breakfast and then got ready for the day's activities.

Zacharias had already left for his day at the Temple.

"We can visit one of our aunts today and then we will stop at the Market Place on the way back. I have some shopping to do", Elisabeth said.

∞∞

"Oh, Mary, do come in. It is so good to see you", Aunt Chloe said. She seemed genuinely glad to see her niece. "It is so nice that you could come, too, Elisabeth. Putting on a little weight?"

"Hello, Auntie. I am glad to see you, too", Elisabeth said sarcastically.

Aunt Chloe was even bigger than Mary had remembered. She was reminded of Mary Elizabeth's Aunt Helena.

Mary jumping to her defense stated, "Elisabeth is with child."

"Really!" Chloe was surprised. Her eyes narrowed, "You are a little past bearing age, are you not?"

Mary retorted, "It is a wonderful miracle, I am excited for her and Zacharias.

"Hmmm, you were married just a short while ago", the woman said, wondering why she was not in Nazareth with her husband.

"Yes, I was. I decided I would like to come to Jerusalem to help Elisabeth. She is in her sixth month.

"Are you and your husband arguing already?" was the comment.

Mary was getting a little irritated with the way the conversation was going. "No, Aunt Chloe. We are very happy. He had a lot of work to do, so this was a good time to visit."

"Do stay for lunch. I will have the servants fix something wonderful", Chloe boasted.

"Thank you so much, but we have things to do", Elisabeth excused.

Mary was relieved. She had taken about all she could.

"Tell your mother hello for me and that we will visit as soon as we can. Your Uncle Joel is so busy, you know", Chloe said as she walked the women to the door.

"Thank you, Aunt Chloe, I will", Mary returned.

The three women hugged and Elisabeth and Mary made a hasty exit.

As they got to the gate Elisabeth exclaimed, "I do not know if you were uncomfortable or not but I surely was. I want to go shopping".

Mary just smiled.

ॐ

The Market Place in Jerusalem was exciting but depressing.

There were dirty, disheveled blind men and crippled men laying on the walkways asking for alms. The streets were cluttered and filthy.

Three Roman soldiers went racing through the street on their horses chasing a man. "Get out of the way. We are coming through. Stop, thief!"

The man ducked behind a vendor's tent and watched as the soldiers rode past. The thief then walked calmly in another direction, as if nothing had taken place.

The vendors were yelling and putting their wares in the faces of perspective buyers. The place was dank with the strong odors of dead fish and rotting fruits, vegetables and meat. Mary had a hard time trying to keep from gagging.

Some of the tents had beautiful bolts of material such as Mary had never seen. Wonderful blues, scarlet, greens, yellows and purples. She lingered a little longer than she should have examining the goods. How marvelous it would be to take some of these beautiful items home to her mother.

Next were the tents with incense and perfumes. After having smelled all of the bad odors, the sweet scents were more than a little nauseating. Mary started retching and Elisabeth decided it was time to return to her house. The girl was looking quite wan.

As they rounded a corner, the guards were racing up another street in some other quest.

It was decided that Mary would not go to the Market Place until she was no longer affected by the pungent odors.

❧❧❧

Most days were spent in Elisabeth's garden. She was very proud of her garden. There were a variety of flowers. She also had some vegetables, herbs and much garlic, which kept the bugs away. It was also used in many of the dishes she prepared. Her motto was "You can never have too much garlic."

The garden had a soothing atmosphere. The only noises heard were the twittering of a few birds and now and then a bee buzzing in and out of the flowers.

Elisabeth was getting larger and it was harder for her to get around. That was another good reason for not going too far.

Although it was getting much cooler at night, Zacharias, Elisabeth and Mary would put on shawls and sit on the verandah and watch the stars after supper. This was a pleasant life. Everything was relaxing and tranquil. Mary was contented to be here, but the Festival of Lights could come none too soon. She missed Joseph more and more.

Mary was doing most of the work around the house, which suited her just fine. The two women were becoming closer and closer. They each found a lot to talk about. During the day they would make blankets and other things for the babies. With both of them expecting, they had a lot in common. They always had something to talk about.

There seemed to be a strong bond between the babies also. Yes, they would be cousins, but when one would do somersaults, the other would reciprocate. The women were amazed at the camaraderie between the two youngsters who were not even born yet.

❧❧❧

It was getting close to the Festival of Lights and Mary was looking forward to being with Joseph again. What was he doing? Did he miss her as much as she missed him?

☙❧

Elisabeth retrieved the menorah and Zacharias put oil in it.
This was the first night of the Festival of Lights.
The women covered their heads.
This was also the first Holy Day since Zacharias had lost his voice. Because he was unable to speak, he had written the blessings down and presented them to Elisabeth to read. He felt that because he had written the words that had to be said, that it would be alright if his wife read them, even though she did not hold the Priesthood.
Before the first light was lit she said, "Blessed art thou, O Lord, our God, and King of the universe, who had sanctified us with thy commandments and bidden us to kindle the Lights".
Zacharias lit the shames, or the work light, and with its flame lit the first lamp in the menorah. Then Elisabeth gave the second blessing, "Blessed art thou, O lord, our God, who did wondrous things for our ancestors in times past in this very season. We kindle these lights in honor of thy holy miracles. The lights are sacred. We do not make use of them but only look upon them in order to give thanks to thy great name".
Last of all, she gave the third blessing, "Blessed art thou, O Lord, our God, and King of the universe, who has kept us alive and well and allowed us to reach this season".
Next Zacharias took the menorah and set it in the window. He then went to a cubbyhole and brought out two gifts, one for Elisabeth and one for Mary.
Elisabeth opened hers first. It was a beautiful comb for her hair made from whalebone. It was the most exquisite comb she had ever seen.
Then Mary opened hers. It was ointment to keep her skin supple so she would not get stretch marks as her abdomen got larger. Zacharias was so thoughtful.

Elisabeth then went to her room and returned with her gifts. First she gave Zacharias his. It was a wonderful robe to use in the temple. She had made it during the summer. He was very pleased.

Mary opened hers. Elisabeth gave her a pair of baby stockings she had knitted for her the week before. Mary had thought they were for her baby cousin. She had so admired them. Tears came to her eyes.

Mary then went to her room and brought her gifts out. First she gave Zacharias his. He opened it with elation, a new yarmulke. The one he wore was ten years old and was showing visible signs of wear. He immediately put it on.

She handed the other gift to Elisabeth. As she opened it she gasped. The beautiful blanket she had helped Mary make. She was so pleased, she was speechless. All she could do was hug the guest.

After the ceremony was over, they ate supper.

On the other seven nights, the third blessing was eliminated and only the first two were said. But each night another candle was lit until they were all lit. Gifts were also exchanged on the remaining nights.

When the Festival of Lights was over, Elisabeth took to her bed. Her strength was gone and Mary was worried about her. It was visible that Zacharias was worried also even though he could not communicate the fact.

He no longer went to the Temple to perform his duties. He did not leave his wife's side. He knew that her time was near.

On the third night after the Festival was over, Elisabeth was laying on her couch when all of a sudden she grabbed her abdomen and gave out a shriek. Mary knew what was happening and sent Zacharias for the midwife.

By the time the midwife arrived with Zacharias, Elisabeth was in anguish. Mary was mopping her sweaty face as the mother-to-be was tossing her head violently.

The midwife asked for clean rags and for Zacharias to leave the room. This was going to be a long night. Zacharias paced all night long. He could hear Elisabeth breathing hard and every so often she would cry out in pain.

Mary stayed in the room with her cousin and continued to put cool, damp cloths on her forehead and to mop up the sweat from her face and neck. Mary agonized with every contraction Elisabeth had. They were coming more frequently now.

As the sun was coming up, Elisabeth could feel the baby's head pushing its way out. She was in a sitting position next to the bed. It was time.

With the next contraction she pushed with all her might. The mid wife was stationed below Elisabeth when the head emerged. The woman held the head firmly and gently turned the baby so that it was in the birthing position.

One more push was all it took. John had arrived.

Mary helped Elisabeth lay on the bed. She was exhausted. It had been a tremendous ordeal.

The midwife held the babe by the legs and gave him a firm swat on the buttocks. He gave out a blood-curdling cry and the woman quickly cleaned the mucous out of his mouth and washed and salted his body and wrapped him in clean cloths. He was then handed to his mother to suckle.

Mary ran and got blankets to cover Elisabeth so she would not go into shock.

The midwife went to the door and beckoned Zacharias to come and see his new son.

„›‹

The soliloquy given by Mary on pp. 132 and 133 was taken from the New Testament KJV Luke1:46-55
Zacharias' vision is found in the New Testament KJV Luke 1:11-20
The Festival of Lights is now called Hanukkah, which is celebrated in December. The references for the ceremony was found in the book: "Hanukkah", by Norman Simon
For the description of the birth of John, I used the book "Celebrating Life: Jewish Rites of Passage", by Malka Drucker

CHAPTER
NINE

Mary Elizabeth was anxious for Mary's return to Nazareth. She had missed her even more than she had thought she would.

She knew that Joseph was making plans to leave soon to get his wife and wished she could go with him. It would seem like an eternity until she would actually arrive.

The girl had kept busy keeping her house clean and planting flower seeds around the rock, shopping, and visiting friends, her parents and John's parents. Time had really gone fast, but not fast enough for her.

❧❧

About a week ago she had had another dream. This time she told no one of it except John.

In her dream she saw a cave which turned out to be a tomb for burial. There was a big rock rolled by it to cover the opening. Soldiers, who were stationed near the rock, were sleeping with their swords nearby.

The rock moved and a man walked out of the tomb.

The soldiers, seeing the rock had been moved, looked into the cave. It was empty. The men became so frightened that they picked up their weapons and ran away, never looking back.

Soon two women came to the tomb with what looked like bottles of oil and jars of ointments for burial.

When they saw that the tomb was empty one of the women left.

The other just sat and cried.

⤫

Then Mary Elizabeth awoke.

She was troubled by this dream as with the others. She did not want to wake John so she went into the other room.

She knelt down and with hands clasped, she looked up toward the ceiling and began to pray.

[Lord, God of heaven and earth, I, thy unworthy servant, come before thee in humble supplication.

There has to be a reason why I am having these dreams. Am I to be the Chosen One as everyone believes? I do not feel worthy of such an honor.]

The girl sat for a few moments contemplating what she would say next, when she heard a quiet voice say, "Mary Elizabeth".

"Here I am", she replied looking around, thinking she had disturbed John.

No one was there.

"Here I am. Lord, is that you?"

"Mary Elizabeth, it is I", the voice said. "Listen carefully to what I have to say. You are not the 'Chosen One'.

"Why am I having these dreams, Lord? Who are they about?" she asked.

"You have been chosen by me to be a Prophetess. The dreams are to guide you.

"You will be instrumental in bringing my Gospel to light. You will be a messenger to my people.

"The visions you have had are of Me. I will be born soon in the town of Bethlehem of a virgin named Mary. She is a chosen vessel unto me.

"Keep yourself pure before me and I will guide you and tell you what you must do."

Mary Elizabeth had her head bowed now. She durst not look. She did not know if the Lord were in the room or only a voice. All she could do is what he told her she must.

"You will be my herald. You must tell everyone you see that the Savior will be born right after Passover is completed. And that they will know it has happened when they see the new star in the heavens.

"I will be the Savior of the world. I will not come with the sword, but with peace and love. The Gospel will teach the people that they must love one another and be forgiving.

"The Law of Moses will be fulfilled in me. The law of repentance and justice will come into force. No more 'eye for an eye' and 'Tooth for a tooth'. Instead, it will be 'Do unto others as you would have them do unto you'.

"By the will of my Father I will heal the sick and afflicted, cast out devils and do all manner of miracles as I have shown you in dreams. Some will esteem me as a great prophet. Others will look upon me with scorn and call me a fake and a blasphemer.

"I will sweat great drops of blood in agony to atone for all of the sins of the world. Not just for the sinners today, but also for the sinners from the beginning of time until the end comes. Only the Son of God could withstand that kind of torture. I will sacrifice my life so that man might live with me in the eternities."

Mary Elizabeth felt humbled and unworthy by the fact that the Lord was talking to her. How could she be worthy to be the messenger of the Lord's Gospel?

"Keep yourself unspotted from the world. Do not envy. For he who covets is a sinner. Do not gossip or even listen to idle gossip. For a gossiper is no better than a covetous person. Follow my commandments, which will be taught to you from time to time. "Above all, love everyone. Be not a respecter of persons. "I leave you now. Be not slothful in doing my work."

He was gone.

Mary Elizabeth awakened her husband.

"Mary Elizabeth, it is still dark outside. I need to sleep longer."

"John, I have had a visit from the Lord."

Her husband was not surprised. He knew of all the dreams she had had in the past. "What did he say?"

Mary Elizabeth told him all that had been said. He was awestruck. He was a bit saddened that they would not be the parents of the Messiah, but he knew their time would come that they would have many children. Now all he could think about was: His Mary Elizabeth-a Prophetess.

Mary Elizabeth set out as soon as she was able, letting everyone she came in contact with know that the Messiah would be born soon in Bethlehem and that the Great Star would be the sign that the event had taken place. Most did not believe her. She was scoffed; she was jeered as she walked about the village.

What was the reason that they would not believe her? She would not lie. She could not lie about this. This was the most important event in all of history. Why would they not believe her?

People could not understand why she would make up such lies. They had been waiting for the Messiah for generations. Why would she be the one to bring the message? No, she could not be believed on this account. She had always been such a good girl. Now she was telling tales that were not true. If she did not stop this foolishness, she would be ostracized or stoned for blasphemy.

Now what was she to do? She was commanded to tell everyone she meets or speaks with about the Gospel or the "Good News". How could she do that if no one would believe her? She thought the task was going to be an easy one, but it turned out to be the most difficult undertaking she had ever faced. She must continue, however. No one told her it would be easy. I guess she would just have to persevere no matter what people said. She knew she was doing the Lord's will.

∽∘∾

The account of the tomb and the women finding the Savior missing is found in the New Testament KJV Matt. 27:60-66, Mark 16:1-4, Luke 23:51-56 and 24:1-3, John 19:38-42 and 20:1-2, "Jesus The Christ" by James E. Talmage, Chapter35 pp. 664-666
The soldiers at the tomb: "Jesus The Christ" by James E. Talmage, Chapter 37 p.678

CHAPTER
TEN

Joseph was just finishing the crib he had made for the Holy Child. Mary would be surprised. He had really outdone himself this time. This was even better than the one he had made for the family in Sapporo. He had engraved apple blossoms across the curved head and foot of the bed. It was highly admired by everyone who came into the shop. He truly was an artist.

He had pretty much caught up on his work and was about ready to leave for Jerusalem. He would leave tomorrow. There was a caravan in the village today that was headed for the Holy City. He would travel with them. It was always better to stay close to people when traveling. There were a lot of marauders out there who would think nothing of raping a woman just because they could or of killing a man for his valuables. If there were no treasures to be had, the man would be killed just because he happened to be in the wrong place at the wrong time.

Joseph had talked to Mary Elizabeth to tell her that he would be leaving soon to accompany Mary back home. The girl was excited about the prospects of having her best friend home again. It had been three *long* months.

Mary Elizabeth had told him of the "Good News". Of the Messiah's birth and some of the prophecies she had received. She was happily surprised when he stated that he believed her.

Of course he believed her. However, he could not tell her that Mary's child would be the Messiah. But he held this in his heart.

The caravan was ready to leave as soon as it was dawn and Joseph was also ready. It had been a long time since he had seen his Mary. She must be getting quite large with the child by now. He could only imagine.

In his dreams and in his memory he could see her ruby red lips, the large brown eyes, and her long brown hair that had the fragrance of jasmine and the luster of the stars. He could see her sweet girlish smile. Yes, he definitely missed her.

The gossip in the village did not bother him. He knew the truth and he loved her more than any words could say. He knew that she was about as near to perfection as any human could get.

"Joseph?" Mary Elizabeth was there just as the camel train was ready to leave.

"Mary Elizabeth, how good of you to see me off." Joseph was truly surprised to see her.

"Please have a safe trip and tell Mary that I miss her very much and do come back soon", the friend said.

"I cannot stay away too long. I still have much to do here", Joseph stated, "We will return very soon."

⤻∘⤸

Mary had awakened early. Baby John had cried because he was hungry. She did not mind being awakened by the baby, though. She knew she would be hearing that a lot in just a few short months. Besides, she wanted to walk to the gate to see if Joseph was coming. He should be arriving soon.

No sign of him yet. She had a lot to keep her busy, though. Elisabeth was much stronger, but still needed help. Anyway, Mary was learning firsthand how to care for a baby. Something some girls did not learn until they had their own, unless they were fortunate enough to take care of younger children in the family. Being the youngest in her family, she had missed that opportunity.

Mary had been to the gate several times a day since the Festival of Lights.

She hoped that her husband would be there tomorrow. That was the day Zacharias and Elisabeth would take John to be circumcised.

Joseph and Mary had been invited.

Mary went back into the house to start the day's chores.

⤻∘⤸

The sun was starting to set and Mary felt a little chilled. She had been enjoying the birds and flowers in Elisabeth's garden. It was almost time for supper and Zacharias would be home soon.

As Mary entered the eating area she was feeling a little depressed. She was hoping this would be the day that Joseph would come, although, she wished that every day. She had looked for him every day for a week. Each evening would be a little more discouraging. Would he never come? Maybe he had not gotten caught up on his work yet. He *did* have a lot to do.

It was almost too late for him to come yet today. If he were on his way, he would probably be stopping for the evening about now.

It would be too dangerous for animals to travel in the dark. The roads were too hard to see. If the animal being ridden or driven should step in a hole or stumble on a rock, a person might fall off and get hurt. Even the animal might break a leg and have to be put out of its misery. That would leave the rider without transportation.

When the meal was over, everyone decided to sit on the verandah. The baby had been fed and would be sleeping soon. His cradle was close to the door so that if he fussed he could be heard. It was totally dark now as they sat watching the peaceful sky. No one said a word. There was no need.

Suddenly they heard a rap at the front door. It was not unusual for someone to call at this hour. Zacharias went to answer the knock. A man's voice was heard.

Mary sat forward in her chair. Could it be? It was much too late for travel. Zacharias and Elisabeth had many friends. Maybe it was one of them.

The girl sat back in the chair and looked again at the sky.

Elisabeth touched Mary's arm softly. The younger woman looked at her cousin who was grinning.

Mary did not know if she dared turn to look. What if it was not Joseph? With apprehension she turned slowly and saw her husband standing with Zacharias.

"Joseph!" Mary shrieked.

All it took was one leap and she was in his strong, capable arms with hers wrapped tightly around his neck kissing him all over his face. And he was reciprocating.

శింోకి

Today John was eight days old. Elisabeth, with the help of Mary, scurried to accomplish the things that needed to be done in order that John could be taken to the High Priest to be circumcised.

Elisabeth, with John wrapped tightly, Zacharias, Mary and Joseph walked to the Synagogue where the ordinance would be performed.

The Priest called for the baby to be brought forth. He made the initial cut with Zacharias holding the infant who was screaming and squirming.

Then the Priest said, "His name shall be called Zacharias after his father".

Immediately, Elisabeth spoke up to the amazement of the men, "Not so. He shall be called John".

And one of the men said to her, "There has never been anyone in your family with that name".

The men then looked at Zacharias and made signs with their hands as if he were deaf as well as dumb.

Zacharias then motioned to the men to bring him a writing tablet. On the tablet he wrote, "His name shall be called John".

Right away he began to speak and to prophesy and to give the child a blessing saying, "Blessed be the Lord God of Israel; For he has visited and redeemed his people, and has raised up a horn of salvation for us in the house of his servant, David as he spoke by the mouth of his holy prophets, which have been since the world began that we should be saved from our enemies, and from the hand of all that hate us; to perform the mercy promised to our fathers, and to remember his holy covenant, the oath which he swore to our father Abraham; that he would grant to us that we, being delivered out of the hand of our enemies might serve him without fear in holiness and righteousness before him all the days of our life.

"And you, child, shall be called the prophet of the Highest. For you shall go before the face of the Lord to prepare his ways. To give the knowledge of salvation to his people by the remission of their sins through the tender mercy of our God; whereby the dawn from on high was visited us to give light to them that sit in darkness and in the shadow of death, to guide our feet into the way of peace."

Everyone was awestruck. To hear such words from a man who until this very moment had been dumb. It was a miracle.

As the family walked back to the house Joseph said, "Zacharias, that was the most beautiful blessing I have ever heard. That is a very special child you have. You should be very proud".

"I am and always will be proud of our son. He is a blessing from God, our own little miracle. The words I said were from Jehovah. I had nothing to do with it", Zacharias said humbly.

The rest of the walk home was quiet. No one said another word.

Joseph took Zacharias aside and quietly stated, "Mary and I will be leaving in the morning".

Zacharias was heartbroken. He had enjoyed having Mary visit them. He was hoping to get to know Joseph a little better.

"Must you leave so soon? Please say you will stay until after the next Sabbath", the older man said.

"I want to get Mary safely back to Nazareth. She is getting large with the child she is carrying and the trip will be difficult for her. I really think we should go.

"In the Synagogue, I heard a man talking about a group of people who are traveling past Nazareth. I thought this would be a good opportunity to leave. I am sure we can travel with them if we get to the highway on time."

As morning light approached, Joseph was already hitching up the donkey. Mary was dressed and was ready. She had packed some food for the trip.

"Elisabeth, Zacharias, I am truly going to miss you", Mary stated. "You both have been so good to me. I know you are family, but I feel closer to you than I ever could have before. I love you both very deeply.

"Take care of John. Give him a big kiss from his cousin, Mary. He is a very special child."

"We know he is", Elisabeth confirmed. "We will tell him all about you and your visit as he is growing up.

"We will miss you too, dear. You have been so much help for me. I do not know what I would have done without you."

Zacharias was weeping openly, "Mary, take good care of yourself, Joseph and especially that little one within your womb. May I give you two a blessing before you leave?"

Joseph looked at the elder man with love and said, "Of course. We would be honored".

The two knelt on the ground in front of Zacharias. He placed a hand on each of their heads and said, "May the God of Heaven look down upon you and may He smile upon you and give you a multiplicity of blessings. May you have a fruitful and prosperous life?

"May this child, who is in the womb. Bring you joy and happiness. There will be much trial and tribulation for each of you, but in the end you will find the happiness and joy that only Jehovah can give you. The child is choice above all men on the earth. He will be known as the Redeemer of the world, the Prince of Peace, the Everlasting Father and also a Man of Sorrows", which was said in almost a whisper as his voice cracked. "He will shed many tears on behalf of his people, Israel. He will be a blessing not only to Israel, but to you also. You are choice beyond measure, because you have been chosen to bring the Messiah into this wicked world.

"You will have much happiness and much sorrow in the days to come.

"I bless you with a safe journey home. May you have peace and much love in your home? May you be blessed with many sons and daughters? Amen.

The two arose and with tears in their eyes, they kissed their cousin on both cheeks.

"Thank you so much. That blessing means a lot to Mary and to me", Joseph said tenderly.

"We must be leaving now. We have a long journey ahead of us."

Joseph placed his hands under Mary's arms and lifted her upon the donkey.

Mary said, "Please let me walk to the meeting place. There will be enough time for riding".

The girl then ran to Elisabeth and threw her arms around her. She gave her a big hug and kissed her on the cheek. "I love you two. Take care. I am sure we will see you again."

With tears streaming down her face, she walked to Joseph and motioned for the trek to begin. She did not look back again. Joseph glanced back long enough to wave good-bye to the loving people.

Joseph and Mary arrived at the designated place just as the sun was peaking over the tree tops. No one could be seen in either direction.

Next to the highway was a fallen log. Mary was already tired, so they sat and talked while waiting for the entourage.

"Mother and Father are well?" Mary inquired.

"Yes they are well. They send their love and are awaiting our return", Joseph answered.

"Joseph", Mary sounded worried, "Is there still a lot of gossip about us?"

"Some." Joseph tried to minimize it. "They just do not understand. And I cannot tell them". Joseph continued, "It is hard to keep a secret like this when people are so negative."

"It will be hard to have to listen to all that talk again. I have been away from it for so long. It has really been a relief", Mary said candidly.

"I knew it was hard on you, that is one of the reasons I wanted you to visit with Zacharias and Elisabeth, even though I knew I would miss you so much" Joseph confessed.

"I missed you, too. Elisabeth did her best to keep me occupied and my mind off of you as much as possible. We made baby clothes and blankets for our babies. They are beautiful.

"We visited my aunts. Most of them were cordial, although Aunt Chloe was quite curt. We left there as soon as we were able and went shopping."

"Shopping? I was working my fingers to the bone and you were shopping?" Joseph teased.

"Yes, but I was sick from all of the smells and we had to go back to Elisabeth's home", Mary said.

"Then you did not buy anything?" Joseph questioned.

"Only a yarmulke for Zacharias for the Festival of Lights", Mary returned, "and something for you. But that is a secret. I will not give it to you until we get home."

"You little tease. Well, I have something for you when we get home, too. And it is also a secret."

Mary hung her head and looked up at him with a little pout on her face.

"That will do you no good. You have to wait until we get home. "By the way, Mary Elizabeth sends her love."

"How is she doing? Is she with child, yet? I sure have missed her."

"I do not know that she is expecting", Joseph said thoughtfully and then continued, "Neither she nor John have said anything to that effect. She kept begging me to come and get you."

"Is she still having dreams?"

"Yes. She also had a visit one night from an angel or someone. She was told that she is not to be the mother of the Messiah and that she is a Prophetess. He gave her a message to tell all the people she comes in contact with that the time is at hand for the Savior to be born and that he would be born in Bethlehem to a virgin named Mary.

"How is that going to be? I am not planning to go to Bethlehem. I do not have a reason to go there. Does she know that I am *that* Mary?"

"I do not think so. She did not seem to indicate that when I spoke with her.

"I really do not think we will be going to Bethlehem. I fear that a journey like that would be too hard on you anyway." Joseph acknowledged.

Mary's husband looked down the highway, "It looks like the mules are coming. We had better be ready".

❧❧

The account of John's circumcism is found in the New Testament KJV Luke 1:59-64
Zacharias' Prophesy is found in the New Testament KJV Luke 1:68-79

CHAPTER
ELEVEN

Even though it was nighttime, Abraham decided to go to the sheep pen and check on the boys and the sheep. He had had an uneasy feeling all evening. He had heard wolves howling in the distance for several nights. He had not revealed it to his wife, but the boys had told him that there had been a pack of wolves hanging close the last couple of nights. It is true that there were five boys, but would they be able to fend off the wolves? Abraham was not aware if there were three wolves or ten. Any more than three and the boys probably would not be able to protect the herd.

"Take Abby with you", Theresa insisted. She did not like to have her men out alone in the dark. She would feel much better if Abby were with her husband.

"The boy is sleeping. There is no sense in disturbing him. I will not be long", the man said reassuringly.

Abraham lit a lantern, took his cloak, the dog and his staff and went out the door.

The night was especially dark. The moon and the stars were covered by a thick layer of clouds. It made it difficult to see the ruts in the road even though he had taken the lantern. Abraham had to walk carefully so he would not trip.

As he moved along, he could hear howling in the distance. All he could think about was that the wolves were there and they were trying to get his sheep.

The dog also heard the wolves and started growling. Abraham bent down and was going to pet him to calm him down when he could feel the hair on his neck stand on edge. Suddenly the dog ran across the field as fast as he could.

Abraham could not go that direction because he was not as sure-footed as the dog. He had to travel by way of the road.

Several of the ewes would be ready to drop babies in another month or so. They would not be able to move quickly enough to stay away from the beasts. In the pen there was not any place to hide.

The shepherd moved a little faster. He had to get to the pen as fast as he could. He could now hear the bleating of the sheep and the growling and gnashing of the canines. The sheep sounded panicky.

He hastened his footsteps again. He must protect his flock.

As he drew nearer, he could hear the boys yelling. The sheep were crying out in agony.

It sounded like the dog had reached the pen. Abraham could hear growling and yelping.

Abraham started running.

"Ahhg." He had fallen as he tripped on a rock in the middle of the road. He had traveled this road a million times, so it seemed, and should have known the rock was there. But it was so dark and so difficult to see.

The pain in his right ankle was excruciating. How could he go on? But he must.

With the staff, he lifted himself up and limped onward toward the commotion on the hill in front of him. He must hurry!

[I have to keep going. I must keep telling myself that my ankle is fine and that it does not hurt very much. Those boys are depending on me. My sheep are depending on me and they will not have a chance if I do not hurry.]

With all the strength he could muster, he ran up the hill to the pen.

When he arrived all he could see was blood and angry, ravenous wolves and the dead dog laying in the corner.

He jumped over the fence into the pen without giving any thought to his aching ankle and started beating off the wolves with his staff.

As he climbed in, the stench of the blood, flesh and wool was nauseating.

Where were the boys? They were not there. Where would they go?

Several wolves were already devouring some of the dead sheep. Others were eating away at the flesh of the still lives ones. They paid little attention to the shepherd. One man was not much of a threat to that many wolves.

All of the sheep would be killed if Abraham did not do something fast. He opened the pen and let the sheep that were still alive out to run. The wolves were busy with the ones who could not get away.

Automatically, he started beating the wolves to get them off of the dead and wounded sheep. He battered them as hard as he could. One fell dead next to one of the lambs. Suddenly, the beasts turned on him. They cornered him. He saw their blood laden gnashing teeth come at him. There was nothing he could do. He covered his head to no avail. They were more than he could deal with. He was one man, alone...

↪↩

Theresa was wide awake because it worried her when Abraham went out so late at night, especially by himself. She was startled out of her deep thought by the sound of beating on the door.

When she opened the door there stood the five shepherd boys. "Where is your husband? There are many wolves in the sheep pen. I am afraid the whole herd will be eaten", the oldest boy said frantically.

Abby appeared rubbing his eyes, "What is going on? Where is Papa?"

"Your father has gone to check on the sheep. He seemed worried when he left. I now know why", Theresa said. All she could do was stare at the door, expecting Abraham to be here. Now she was starting to panic.

"We were told this morning that there have been wolves hanging around the last couple of nights. We did not see or hear any signs of

127

them when we were out in the day. And I thought the boys could handle it", Abby stated. "It must be that Papa did not think so.

"Let me get my sandals and I will go back with you."

All of the boys, with Abby in the lead, ran as fast as they could up the hill. No sound was coming from the pen. The majority of the sheep were in the field grazing.

Silently, the six youth crept up to the pen. They grabbed the torches which were kept burning at night. They went carefully into the pen not knowing what they might find.

There in the flickering light they could see about eight sheep torn in shreds and mostly devoured.

One of the boys quickly pushed Abby out the gate of the pen. "You do not want to see this."

Abby pushed the boy aside and stepped inside the gate. In the corner lay what remained of Abraham. He had been mangled pretty badly by the wolves. His face was unrecognizable. His clothes were a mass of blood. His eyes were open as if he were staring off into the distance. In another corner lay the dead dog.

Abby screamed, grabbed his mouth and quickly made his way out of the gate and gagged and vomited where he stood.

ॐ

In the distance Mary and Joseph could begin to make out the village of Nazareth. What a welcome sight; the Synagogue on the top of the hill and the homes and shops.

Mary was exhausted. It had been a long, tiring trip. It was amazing the difference three months could make. Three months ago, the trip to Jerusalem had been fun and exciting. She was not at all this tired when she reached Elisabeth's house. Now, all she wanted to do was lie on her own bed and rest for a week.

As they reached the village there was an eerie feeling in the air.

Something was definitely wrong.

They went to their house. Joseph gently lifted Mary off the donkey. She was sore all over. It would feel good to lie on a bed once again.

Joseph brought in the things from the trip and carefully laid them on the floor in the main room. Then he walked quietly into the bedroom and in almost a whisper said, "Mary, you rest. I am going to take the donkey back to the stable and then go to the shop and see what is happening there".

Mary did not respond. She just smiled.

Joseph closed the entrance door quietly and headed for the carpentry shop. As he was nearing Abraham and Theresa's home he heard wailing and moaning. What was going on?

He walked to the open door and looked in. About eight women, whom he knew, were in the attitude of mourning.

Upon entering the house, Mary Elizabeth ran to him and threw her arms around him. "Oh, Joseph, it is Papa. He is dead. What am I going to do without my papa?" the girl sobbed.

All Joseph could do was stand and hold his wife's best friend tight. He did not want to ask any questions of the girl. That would only complicate things. There was enough commotion without his adding to it.

John came across the room and stood before the two who were embracing. He gripped Joseph's shoulder firmly and said sorrowfully, "Joseph, I am glad you are home."

With that, Mary Elizabeth let go of Joseph and was in her husband's arms.

"We just arrived", Joseph said softly. "What happened?"

John gently set his wife to his side. "Come outside where we can talk."

Mary Elizabeth did not mind. She was tired of hearing the tragic story. She would go and sit by her mother. Maybe she could be of some comfort to her.

The two men walked outside. "How is Mary? You did bring her back?" John inquired.

"I brought her home. She is resting at our house. The journey was very hard on her. She is exhausted.

"What happened to Abraham?"

John began slowly, choking back the tears, "He was killed by wolves a few nights ago. He went to the pen to check on the sheep. There was a whole pack, maybe ten.

"The shepherds ran to get Abraham. They must have crossed each other somewhere in the field. They did not know that Abraham was already on his way. There was nothing that could be done. There were just too many of the wolves.

"Abraham must have opened the pen and let the sheep out because all of the dead sheep were in the pen and the others were in the field", John explained and then continued. "All that was in the pen was about eight dead and partially eaten sheep, Abraham and his dead dog. They were dead by the time the boys returned with Abby, and the wolves were gone. I could see where a couple of sheep had been dragged away."

"You were there, too?" Joseph said surprised.

"After it was all over, Abby ran to our house and woke us up. Mary Elizabeth ran to comfort her mother and I went to the scene of carnage. It was awful. I looked the situation over and assessed the damage.

"Abby and I took the dead carcasses out of the pen along with the dog and Abraham. We set them beside the pen and then rounded up the remaining sheep and herded them back into the pen and locked it up.

"The shepherds were frightened and would not stay with the sheep. They all went back to their respective villages." "Who stayed with the sheep?" Joseph inquired.

"No one at first. Abby and I took Abraham home and took care of things there. Then later, I went back out to the pen to watch over the sheep.

"It was not likely that the wolves would be back. I am sure they had had their fill."

"Has anyone found the wolves?" Joseph asked.

"No. We have put traps out, hoping to catch them. But we have not had any luck, so far", John replied.

"What about finding some more shepherds? That is a task that will not be easy. Now that the master has been killed, no one will want to take the risk", Joseph stated.

"I know. Abby cannot stay by himself day and night with the sheep. It is a rough situation, one that will take a while to work out.

"We have been to a couple of villages. We even tried to talk some of the boys, who were here, into coming back. That did not work. They are scared to death. They are afraid that the wolves will be back and they will end up like Abraham. We told them we would kill the wolves, but that did not matter. No amount of persuasion will bring the boys back."

"I am sorry all this has happened", Joseph said apologetically. "Is there anything Mary and I can do?"

"I think it would mean a great deal if Mary could come by for a visit. That is, if she is not too tired."

"I will talk with her about it when I get home. It has been good to see you. I just wish it could have been under better conditions."

The two men cupped each other on the shoulder. One went back to into the house and the other walked toward the carpenter's shop.

&⁕⸲

"Son, it is so good to see you. When did you arrive home?" Heli asked.

"About an hour ago, I just came from Abraham's house", Joseph stated.

"Then you know", the father said sadly.

"Yes, it is tragic. The family is going to have a hard time.

"Mary Elizabeth is taking it badly, I am sorry to say."

"Have you told Mary yet?" Heli asked.

"No. I have to go home and do that now. It is going to be hard on her. He was like a second father to her." With that, Joseph was gone.

As he walked to his door he had a sinking feeling. Telling his wife about Abraham was going to be the hardest thing he has ever done.

When he opened the door, Joseph was face to face with Mary and Mary Elizabeth. They were sitting with their arms around each other sobbing.

Joseph was embarrassed. He did not know quite what to say to the women. Mary knew. There was nothing more he could do for her at the moment. The two women were comforting each other.

"Mary, if you are all right, I am going back to Theresa's house to see if I can be of help to John".

Mary gave him half a grin through her tears.

தை௸

After the period of mourning was over and the burying done, the village tried to get back to normal.

Abby and John had been fairly unsuccessful in finding help with the sheep. They were able to find only a couple of shepherds.

The wolves had not been caught, but they had not been around bothering Abby or the other shepherds, either. All seemed calm... too calm.

The new shepherds were a little older and wiser. They were more professional at taking care of sheep than the younger boys had been. It would cost more to pay them, but in a long run it would be worth it. They would be more dependable. At least they would not be quite as afraid of wolves and other hazards.

Some amount of caution should always be taken around wild Animals, but the men were more experienced and knew how to handle such situations with more confidence.

Until a few more shepherds could be added, John was helping at night after working a full day at the bakery. Luckily, he could get *some* sleep because one of the shepherds, named Simon, was a very capable man. John would sleep a little while and then check to be sure that all was well.

If they could find at least one additional good shepherd John could stay home and get a full nights rest. That would make Mary Elizabeth happier. She worried about John not getting enough sleep at night and then working all day. She feared that he might have an accident and would not be any good to his father or Abby.

Since his father had died, Abby now wanted to be called Abraham. His mother complied with pride. He was really proving himself to be the man that he had always tried to convince everyone that he was.

క్రూజ్

Mary Elizabeth was becoming concerned because she had not conceived as yet. She knew she should not be, because they had only been married a few months. But Mary had been with child for some time and was getting very large and spoke of the child moving within her and of her dreams and aspirations for the babe, all the while working on baby garments.

It saddened Mary Elizabeth that she was not experiencing the same things as her friend as they worked together.

She was keeping busy, though. She was trying to keep her mind on other things. But it was difficult when she spent so much of her time with Mary.

Seeing the light which shone in her friend's eyes as she spoke of the child in her womb, caused much pain for Mary Elizabeth, although, she tried not to show it. She really *was* happy for Mary, even though, at the same time being envious.

She was still trying to spread the "Good News" that the Christ Child would soon be born, but to no avail. It almost always fell on deaf ears. Most would not believe it. Even the Rabbi did not. He felt that if it were going to happen soon, the message would come through someone with more authority. Mary Elizabeth was a "woman". How would she know about such an important event? Why would it be revealed to her? She did not hold the Priesthood of Aaron. It would definitely come from someone in the Priesthood. No, it would not be told to a mere woman.

Even her mother was skeptical, although, she wanted to believe. She always knew that her daughter was more than just a woman. She was definitely more. But a Prophetess who claimed to speak to

133

God? She was not sure that this could be true. He had never spoken to *her*. And besides, if she was a Prophetess, why was she not warned of her father's impending accident and death. No, she could *not* be a Prophetess. She must be hallucinating.

Mary Elizabeth quit trying to convince those who would not believe. She only spoke about it to those who hoped she was right.

She talked much about it to Mary. *She* believed her. *She* did not think that Mary Elizabeth was being foolish.

They talked long hours about the event and what it might mean to the troubled world.

Yes, Mary had always understood her friend. Mary Elizabeth could tell her *anything*.

⁍

Just before Passover, a garrison of Roman Soldiers rode into the village. People came out of their shops and homes to see what the soldiers were doing there.

They rode straight to Simon's Inn and entered. The men ordered refreshment and sat and laughed as they drank their ale and spoke of their journeys together. They did not converse with the innkeeper or anyone else except to order another round of the beverage. They were there on a mission.

The soldiers did not care much for the townspeople, anyway. As far as they were concerned, these Israelites were much too opinionated about Roman rules and Caesar, whom they did not seem to want to obey anyway. It appeared to them that the only reason the townspeople obeyed was to keep the peace so they would not be thrown into prison for insubordination and insurrection.

And all this nonsense about waiting for a Messiah to liberate them was foolish. Everyone knew that Caesar Augustus was the only God at this particular time.

As soon as they finished their libations at the Inn, they tacked a piece of paper to the board in front of the building, remounted their horses and slowly rode away.

When the soldiers had disappeared from view, the villagers gathered slowly to read the proclamation.

Hear Ye

All Israel is to be taxed by the order of Caesar Augustus.
When your Passover has been accomplished, each head of household will go to the place of his birth and register with a Roman official. This will be performed in an orderly manner and must be done as soon as your Holy Day is completed. No one will be exempt.

That was straightforward and understood by all. The men would have to leave their families if they had not been born in Nazareth and go to the town or city of their nativity to register to be taxed by Caesar, *again*!

Had they not been taxed enough already? Did they not have enough rules to live by? When would it end? Where was the long awaited Messiah who would free them from the Roman oppression and from the evil tyrant, Caesar? Would he never come?

৵৽

Account of Taxation: The New Testament KJV Luke 2:1

135

CHAPTER
TWELVE

Joseph was concerned about leaving Mary to travel to Bethlehem where he had been born.

"Joseph, you know I must go with you. This child must be born in Bethlehem to fulfill the prophecy."

"Oh, Mary, you are so large and tire so easily these days. How can you make such a long journey?"

"I can do it with your love and help and with the help of Jehovah. He will not let anything happen to me or His Child."

He knew she was right, but he still feared for the safety of his wife and the precious child. He could not help it. He loved her so much. How could he jeopardize her life? She had never been very strong and was especially vulnerable now.

As Passover approached, she rested more and more. Joseph became more and more concerned.

❧◦❧

John, Abraham and the other shepherds looked over the herds with great interest. Only the whitest and purest lambs could be chosen as sacrifices for Passover. There had been many lambs born this year. They would be able to sell numerous little ones to those who did not raise their own.

The lambs were rounded up and washed in the creek nearby. They had to be as clean and beautiful as possible. This took some time because of the enormity of the offspring.

The men slapped each other on the backs and congratulated one another for the accomplishment. The lambs would be more than suitable sacrifices.

The herd was separated and the clean, snowy white young lambs were put into holding pens by themselves where they awaited inspection by the purchasers. Some came from nearby villages because they knew Abraham's lambs were always among the best anywhere. Thanks be to Jehovah, this would be completed in a couple of days.

It would be harder to watch all of the sheep now because of the split. The shepherds would have to be more wary than usual, especially because the wolves would seek out the lambs. They were more tender and delicious and of course, they couldn't run as fast.

Abraham spent the days before Passover at the pens selling the lambs and tallying the money. He made a handsome profit and shared some of it with his shepherds to show his appreciation to them for a job well done. He had seen his father do the same. It was always a good idea to be a little bit more generous with the hired help at this time of year. It gave them a stronger feeling of loyalty. And besides, good help was hard to find.

The day arrived. Passover, the day which had been celebrated for generations, since that day in Egypt when the children of Israel had spread lambs blood on the doors of their homes so the Destroying Angel would pass over and not kill their first born. The night Pharaoh had decided he had had enough of Moses' plagues and let the Israelite people return to the Promised Land. That blessed day that had been celebrated ever since and ever would be until the Messiah would come and liberate the Promised Children once again.

John prepared to take his lamb to the Synagogue to be slaughtered. People tried to go to Jerusalem to the Temple on this special day. But knowing that the trip would have to be taken soon after the Holy Day, most of the men of Nazareth would stay there.

There were enough Priests to make sure the ritual was performed properly.

In the afternoon, trumpet blasts sounded form the Synagogue. This was the call to sacrifice. Next came the cry of a priest, "People of the Lord, in the name of Him who rests in the Great and Holy House, Listen! The time for slaughtering the Pesach lamb has arrived".

The men brought their sacrifices to the Synagogue. They were taken a few at a time to the place of slaughtering. The men killed their own animals. As they did so, a musician priest sang songs of praise to God.

Besides the paschal offering, there was a second sacrifice. Because Passover was a Holy Day, there was a separate sacrifice for the day itself. This was a hagigah, or holiday sacrifice. They brought grain or cakes of unleavened bread as a second sacrifice. The men then hurried home, carrying the slaughtered animal in its skin, and put it to roast in an oven outside and soon the holiday was under way.

Everyone put on white clothes.

John and Mary Elizabeth celebrated the occasion with Mary Elizabeth's mother, Theresa, and Abraham and Sarah. This was their first Passover without the elder Abraham, so John wanted to be sure that it was done properly. Next year, the younger Abraham would be able to do everything for his family. John had Abraham participate with him in all the rituals, so he could learn how it was to be done. Abraham had seen his father officiate in this ritual many times, but until he had done it himself he was unsure. He wanted to make sure he did it just right as it should be.

People first celebrated at home with the meal and a holiday discussion. A small table with symbolic holiday foods: bitter herbs, matzah, a pudding of mashed fruit and nut called haroset, and two cooked foods was placed before John.

John then explained the meanings of these foods as he told the story of the night of the exodus from Egypt. The pudding stood for the clay the slaves used to make bricks. The matzah stood for the bread the slaves ate in haste the night they left Egypt. The two cooked foods were from the day's two sacrifices; a piece of lamb from the pesach offering and a matzah cake from the hagigah, or holiday offering.

Then, if there were younger children in the house, they would take a short nap.

At midnight everyone went to the Synagogue where, standing up, they ate roast lamb, matzah, and bitter herbs and sang songs of praise to God. The bitter herbs were eaten by putting them between two pieces of matzah.

The people stood as they ate to represent eating in haste so they would be ready to leave Egypt when they were done.

The rabbi then told the people, "On Passover, all Jews should think of themselves as having personally escaped from slavery".

One young boy asked, "Why?"

The rabbi then answered, "You would still be slaves in Egypt if your ancestors had not been set free".

"Everyone, not just the rich, should drink four cups of wine mixed with water during the ceremony.

"No one should be alone on Passover.

"Do not watch the night expecting to see an act of God, because God is present at all times, not only at night. Instead, please God by doing a good deed. Open the door and call out into the street, 'Let all who are hungry, come and eat.'"

After the celebration was ended, all friends would hug and kiss and then go to their respective homes.

ॐ

Everyone always had a good time at Passover, but that was over and the heads of households must prepare to leave for their native cities, unless they were native to Nazareth. They would travel to their destinations together as much as possible. Heli, Jacob, Joseph, John, Benjamin, and Abraham were all from Bethlehem, of the lineage of David, so they would travel together. Others would go in different directions.

ॐ

Mary Elizabeth was invited into Mary's house. "You and I should make some plans as to what we will do while the men are gone."

"I already have plans. I am going with them", Mary explained.

"You cannot. Look how big you are. The baby is due anytime. That would be foolish."

Mary looked at her friend tenderly and stated, "Joseph is worried about me staying home. He would rather have me with him so he can watch over me. He is so good to me. How can I refuse?"

"Well, if you are going I will go too, in case you need help. Besides, the Savior is to be born in Bethlehem about this time. Maybe we will be able to see him", Mary Elizabeth said prophetically.

"You are probably right, but maybe John will not want you to go."

"I *will* go. John will understand", Mary Elizabeth stated emphatically.

"I love you dearly and I am glad that you want to help me, but please do not upset John. I will be fine. Joseph will take good care of me. You know that."

"Yes, I *do* know that, but if there is something I could have done and was not there for you, I would never forgive myself. Besides, I am a woman. What do men know about birthing babies?

"No more arguing. I will go and speak with John now. I will talk to *you* later."

Mary watched as the door shut. Mary Elizabeth was such a wonderful friend. She wished she could tell her the whole truth about why she was going to Bethlehem.

"John", Mary Elizabeth called as she entered the bakery. No one was in sight.

"Here I am. Come back", John said from the back room.

The girl entered the room where her husband was arranging the freshly baked breads. She watched as he carried them with care to the table in the front of the shop and then followed.

"John, I want to go to Bethlehem with you to register."

"Do you think that is wise? With Abraham going, who will watch over your mother?"

"I am sure there is someone who would be more than happy to look in on Mother and Sarah once in a while", Mary Elizabeth returned.

"Why is it so important that you go?" John questioned.

"Joseph wants Mary to go. She is so close to her time that I worry about her. What if she has the baby? Who will take care of the birth? Joseph will not know what to do.

"I was also thinking that if the Messiah were to be born while we are there, maybe I would get to see him", his wife said, so softly that John could barely hear her.

"I can see you are determined. I think everyone will be leaving in the morning. Be prepared for a long boring ride. You know that donkeys are not very comfortable and they travel very slowly." John smiled as he watched the excitement of his wife's face.

Mary Elizabeth ran to her husband and threw her arms around his neck and kissed him tightly. When she released him she said, "Thank you, my darling. I will be prepared for anything."

☙❧

The morning came. The sun rose bight and clear. The scent of the spring flowers wafted in and through the village as a fragrant bouquet.

People were up and about readying for the day's tasks.

In the distance a cloud of dust could be seen. The Roman soldiers were coming to take the census of all the Nazarenes.

The donkeys were braying as the Bethlehemites led them to the center of town to begin the journey to their nativity. They were all there including the two women.

As the soldiers approached the caravan of donkeys, the lead officer halted and held up his right hand as a signal for all to stop.

"Where are you going?" the uniformed man inquired.

"We are on our way to Bethlehem to register. That is the city of our nativity", John stated.

"Why are the women going?" the soldier came back.

"This one", pointing to Mary, "is with child. Her husband wants to be with her when the child is born. My wife', pointing to Mary Elizabeth, "is going as mid-wife."

"That seems a little risky to me, but what is another Jew, more or less."

The soldiers laughed and continued to the other end of town where they would set up their tents first, then begin the task of registering all the Nazarenes for the census.

John lifted Mary Elizabeth onto the first donkey.

John and Joseph had two donkeys each, one for supplies and the other for riding. Most of the men could ride and still have room for supplies. John and Joseph could ride on their second donkeys if they wanted, but for now they would walk.

Carefully, Joseph set his beloved wife on the back of the donkey. "Are you comfortable?"

"Yes, My Love. Do not worry about me. I will be just fine."

Looking to the rear of the train to be sure everyone was ready, John motioned the group forward.

Mary knew this would not be easy. She had made almost the same trip just a few months earlier, except this time they would be going to Bethlehem. There would be many rocky hills to climb. She was already uncomfortable. It would only get worse. But she was determined not to complain. She knew this journey was necessary in many ways.

Joseph would take care of her. She had no reason to worry. She knew the child would not be born before they reached Bethlehem.

❧❧

They had been on the road several days when Joseph could see the anguish in his wife's eyes. He knew she was in agony. They had to stop. She could not go on at this pace with so little rest.

That night Joseph said to John, "Mary and I will stay here for a couple of extra days. She is weary and must get some rest."

"We will send the others on in the morning. Maybe they can acquire a room for us", John suggested.

"You go on with the others. I am sure there will not be many rooms left by the time you arrive. See if you can attain one for us. We will not be far behind. I think we better take it slower for Mary's sake.

"I know this cannot be easy for her, but you must think that it would be better if Mary Elizabeth were with her in case the worst happened?" John said thoughtfully.

"No, you go on ahead. I am sure that if we go slowly it will be all right for Mary".

That night was not a pleasant one. The girls argued as they had not done since they were small children.

"Mary, I need to stay with you. What if you should start laboring?"

"Please go. I will be fine. I just need a little rest. I am sure I will make it to Bethlehem", Mary kept repeating to Mary Elizabeth.

"I cannot leave you. Maybe John could go ahead and get rooms for us so I could be with you."

"No you should be with your husband. I will be alright." And so it went until both women fell asleep.

In the morning the argument continued until finally it was agreed that Mary would only rest one full day and not be far behind the entourage.

Mary Elizabeth was tearful as the girls parted. Mary kept her composure well, although, she really would have liked her friend to stay behind with her. She knew it would be easier for a husband and wife to get a room than a man by himself. The innkeepers would figure a man could fend for himself in a tent somewhere. Maybe if they did get a room, Mary and Joseph could stay in it with them.

The caravan departed. Mary Elizabeth went hesitantly. Mary lay under the shade of the lean-to Joseph had put up every night since their departure from Nazareth. She would rest as best she could today so they could get an early start tomorrow. In two more days they should be in Bethlehem. Then she could give birth to this wonderful Son and rest.

The heat of the day was almost unbearable even though it was still spring. She was thankful for the shelter.

"Mary, would you like a drink of water or a little bread?" Joseph asked trying his best to make sure Mary was comfortable.

"Yes, some water would be nice", she replied in almost a whisper.

As he lifted her head to let her take in the moisture, it was obvious that she was exhausted. She did not have the strength to help herself. Joseph slowly poured drops of water into her mouth as she swallowed carefully.

How could she bare two more days on that donkey? How could she rest when it was so hot? But she must. What if she *should* start laboring before she got there? What could Joseph do? He should have insisted that Mary Elizabeth stay with Mary, too late now. The rest of the group had left early that morning.

The sun would be setting soon. Then it would cool down so that this fragile woman would be able to rest more easily.

As soon as the daylight had departed, Joseph reached into a sack and retrieved some fruit and bread for himself and his wife. However, she was sleeping peacefully. It would not be right to awaken her.

He ate his food and then retired next to Mary. He lay on his side and gently placed his ample hand on her swollen abdomen. No movement from within. "He" must be sleeping, too.

As Joseph lie thinking of the day and the coming event, he could hear wolves somewhere a long way off singing their doleful songs to each other and to the moon. Softly, he began to hum. He remembered a song that his mother used to sing to him when he was a child. A smile came upon his face and he was at ease, even in the desert, lying beside his beautiful wife; the Chosen One, the Woman among Women, the mother of the Savior of the world.

Mary suddenly awoke and sat up with a start. "Joseph, we must leave now!"

"But it is still dark. We will not be able to see. The donkeys might step into a hole and break a leg. We cannot go yet. Why not just rest until daybreak. It will not be too long now. I can see the sky starting to lighten over that hill", he said pointing to the east. He lay back down.

"Joseph, we must leave now." Mary was now sounding panicky. "My time has come. We must get to Bethlehem."

The man just looked at his wife. He was dazed. He knew that it would be soon, but now? He thought he would have plenty of time to get to Bethlehem, rent a room and to make Mary comfortable before she actually began to travail.

"Are you all right?" he asked quietly trying not to upset her.

"I am fine", she replied, "I just know that my time has come. I am not in any pain,… yet. I have this strong urge to get to Bethlehem as fast as possible. I just know that it is time that we must leave."

Joseph gave Mary another sip of water, packed their belongings on one donkey's back and put Mary on the other donkey.

꧁꧂

The noise of Bethlehem was overpowering. John had never seen so many people in this small town. Dogs were running in the street with no apparent place to go. People were sitting by the buildings and next to the roads begging for food and shelter, and trying to shade themselves from the afternoon heat. The stench of sweaty, dirty bodies was unbearable as the group of donkeys moved toward one of the Inns.

The men along with Mary Elizabeth went to the man who was trying to sweep his porch around the lazy bodies.

"Do you have a room for us to lodge in while we are here?" John inquired.

"I do have a place for you to sleep, the Innkeeper shouted, "but you will have to share it with another couple. How long will you be here?"

"Hopefully, we will be here only a couple of days. We do not mind sharing a room. We have friends coming not far behind us. We will share the room with them", John said happily.

"No, you do not understand. The room is already taken. Another couple is already there. You will have to sleep on the floor", the Innkeeper impatiently stated. "Do you want it or not? If you do not, I am sure someone else will. There is no other place available in the city. The men will have to find a place to sleep somewhere else, maybe outside by the donkeys."

"Yes, we will take it", Mary Elizabeth said abruptly before the Innkeeper changed his mind. John just stared at her in amazement. John unpacked the donkey and took Mary Elizabeth to the prepared room. As they looked in, Mary Elizabeth began to sob.

"I wanted the room so that we could share it with Joseph and Mary. I thought there might be room on the floor for them, too."

There was a bed, four blankets spread on the floor and maybe space for John and his wife; that would be crowding it. There would be no room for their friends. She could do nothing by cry.

John left her there to put their blankets down to mark their spot, so they would be assured not to lose their places. Of course, that was not an assurance. Someone *could* move the blanket and claim the space as their own.

John went with the men to find a place for the donkeys, to give them water and provender. The other men would have to find their own places to sleep.

$$\approx\approx$$

It was getting nigh unto sundown. Walking had been slow but steady. Joseph and Mary had not encountered any problems...but it had been slow.

Then Joseph heard a short gasp from Mary. "Is something wrong?"

"No, but we need to keep moving. We must reach Bethlehem this night. We *have* to keep going."

Joseph could see that Mary was tired and uncomfortable. "Are you sure you do not want to stop for the night? We could be in Bethlehem by mid-morning."

"No, mid-morning will be too late. Please keep going." [Oh, no, she is going into labor.]

"How can we? We must stop so you can rest a bit and then go on into Bethlehem."

"We cannot stop. If we do not continue, we will not be in Bethlehem when this child is born", Mary stated as she wrenched in pain.

"Oh, Mary, what can I do? If we stop, the baby will not be born in Bethlehem. If we do not, you may not be able to bear the suffering."

"We must go on to fulfill the prophecy. This baby must be born in Bethlehem", Mary said and then continued, "I will be fine."

As they walked to the top of the next hill they could see the faint lights of Bethlehem. "Only a few more miles and we will be there. Are you all right?

"Do not worry about me. Just keep moving." Mary's head was now hung low. The pain was getting worse, but the end was in sight.

❧❧

"When do you think Mary and Joseph will get here?" Mary Elizabeth asked her husband with anticipation.

"Hopefully, tomorrow sometime", came the answer.

"I will sit outside tomorrow and watch for them. Maybe we will be able to find a place for them", his wife said with great enthusiasm.

"Quiet down! Some people would like to sleep", came a harsh voice from somewhere within the room.

No more was said. After a few minutes, all that could be heard was soft snoring.

❧❧

As Joseph led the two donkeys into Bethlehem, all that could be heard was soft whimpering from his wife. Everyone was sleeping in the town.

He stopped at the first Inn and knocked softly, trying not to disturb too many people. The Innkeeper came to the door and shouted, "There is no room here. Go away and let people sleep." Many people sleeping on the floor just behind the door moaned and complained of the noise.

Joseph said, "My wife is in labor and I must find a soft place for her to rest."

"Git outta here. She should not have come, anyway. You are crazy for bringing her. I said there is no room here." He slammed the door. More complaining was heard from inside the Inn.

Joseph continued on to the next Inn and again knocked softly. The Innkeeper answered and said quietly, but harshly "Get out of here", motioning to the people on the floor. "You must be able to see that we are full! Sleep in the street like the others.

"We cannot. My wife is heavy with child and needs a place to lie."

"Well, it is not going to be here. Besides, we do not need any babies born here. The patrons are trying to sleep."

Before Joseph could say anymore, the door was quietly shut.

There was one more Inn on the far outskirts of town. They must have a place. They cannot all be full.

The two donkeys were resisting the pull that Joseph had on them, trying to get them to keep moving. They were tired, too, but they must continue on their way until a resting place could be found for the couple and the donkeys.

When they got to the last Inn Joseph looked haggard and worn. Poor Mary was in serious travail by this time.

Joseph knocked softly. No one answered. He knocked again a little harder. A kindly looking, old man came to the door. "I am sorry, but we do not have room for you."

Joseph said, "There must be someplace. My wife is laboring in much pain. I must have a place for her to lay her head."

"I wish I could help you, but I know of no place in Bethlehem", he said scratching his head. "The only place I know of is our stable behind the Inn. There is clean straw. There are many animals, but I do not think they would mind sharing that space with you, if *you* do not mind."

"That will be fine. We will find our way", Joseph said gratefully, and then added; "Do you know of a midwife who is close?"

"My wife, Rebekah, is a midwife. Is your wife ready? Yes, I am sure she is", the Innkeeper said as an afterthought as he looked at the mother-to-be. "I will awaken her and send her right out."

"Thank you. You are too generous. I will take my wife to the stable and try to comfort her until your wife comes", Joseph returned.

He led the two donkeys to the rear of the building. There it was, a stable. Was this anyway to bring a baby into the world, especially *this* baby? He should be born in a palace with all of the luxury that kind of lifestyle affords a king. Why would he be born in such a humble place? No one would ever believe that the Son of God would be born in a stable.

As they entered, Joseph surveyed his surroundings. Sure enough, there was clean straw over to one side. It looked as if someone had prepared the place just for them. How could that be?

The animals were all in the back.

Joseph carefully helped his wife off of the donkey. He carried her to the straw. He laid her to one side so he could fluff the hay to make it a little more like a bed. He put a blanket on top and then gently laid Mary on it.

He then unpacked the animals and led them to the back with the others. They found water and drank until it seemed as though they would empty the trough.

Joseph dipped a piece of cloth, which he had retrieved from one of the bags, in some water and went to Mary and mopped her forehead.

"Water, Oh, Joseph, I need a little drink of water", Mary begged.

At that moment a plump little lady entered the stable. "No drinks. Get another piece of cloth and wet it. She can suck on that".

Joseph followed the instructions and laid the wet cloth on Mary's lips. She sucked in the moisture eagerly.

"Did you bring anything for the baby?" Rebekah asked.

Joseph looked confused.

"You know. Swaddling clothes anything? You know the baby must be swaddled", the midwife commented.

"Yes, they are in the bag. I will get them for you."

She gave Joseph a wary look, "Your wife is far along. I do not know how she made it here. How could you make her wait so long? The baby has been ready for some time." She was visibly angry about the whole situation.

She bent down. Mary was not able to get to a sitting position. She was much too weak.

Rebekah bent Mary's legs at the knees with her feet flat on the bed, so that she appeared to be sitting, although, she was in actuality lying on her back.

Joseph was busy getting things out of the bag when he heard, "Would you like to see your son?" The woman's demeanor had changed drastically. The crassness was gone. She was now this soft person with an overabundance of compassion.

The 'earthly father' looked stunned. "Already? I have not had time to get all of the things out."

Rebekah grinned, "Babies do not wait for anyone. When it is their time, they just come. He has not even cried."

Joseph rushed to the side of the midwife, "Is he all right?"

"Look for yourself."

As he peered into the blanket, he could see the baby, wide-eyed and intently watching the moving shadows.

"Is my wife safe?"

"She is tired, but otherwise fine. She is the bravest little mother I have ever seen. She did not make a sound", Rebekah commented.

"I need to clean him and swaddle him. Then we will give him to his mother. He needs to be fed", the woman stated as she started to softly hum a lullaby. Her music was soothing and Mary fell asleep.

Joseph knew that the baby would need a place to sleep while Mary was sleeping, so he looked around and spied a manger that was not being used. He emptied it out and put clean straw in it. He got a clean baby blanket and put it over the straw. This would do nicely.

Suddenly, he looked out the door. There was a bright light. That was strange because it would not be daylight for a couple of hours but it was as light as noonday. He walked to the opening to get a better look at this phenomenon. He walked outside and raised his arm to shade his eyes. He looked above the stable. To his amazement, the biggest, brightest star he had ever seen shone right on the building.

He re-entered the stable and stood still as his eyes got used to the dim light once more. He did not say anything, but he *did* remember what Mary Elizabeth had said about a star over the place of the Messiah's birth, though, and he smiled.

☙❧

"What time do you think Joseph and Mary will arrive?" Mary Elizabeth asked.

"I would not expect them much before sundown", John iterated.

"Well, I am going to watch all day. I do not want to miss them."

"The townspeople have been talking about a star that appeared last night. They said it was the biggest, brightest star they have ever

150

seen and that it seemed to be shining in one particular place on the other side of town", John said, with great excitement.

"It has happened. The Messiah has been born. We must go see him tonight when the star is shining", Mary Elizabeth demanded.

"We can all go."

"It will be so exciting. When we go home we can tell everyone that we saw the Son of God.

"Wait till I tell Mary. This is so thrilling", the girl said with exuberance.

❧

"Joseph is everything all right?" Mary inquired.

"Everything is fine", Joseph assured his wife.

Rebekah was aroused, "How are you feeling this morning, my dear?"

"I am fine, although I am still a little weak. Can I hold my baby?"

"He is awake. I can see him moving his little arms. I will bring him to you. I am sure he is hungry", Rebekah answered. "By the way, have you discussed a name for him? I am tired of referring to him as 'the baby'."

"We will call his name Jesus."

"Well, here is Jesus", she said as she handed the baby to his mother. "What a wonderful child. I still have not heard him cry." The mother and baby slept most of the day.

The star was there even in the day, although, it did not give off much light. At eventide the star shone bright again.

Soon after the sun slid behind the hills, three shepherds appeared at the entrance to the stable. The older one asked, "May we come in? We have come to see the Messiah."

Joseph said, "I do not understand, how did you know?"

"We heard music. When we looked up, from the direction where the music was coming, we saw many angels sing God's praises and giving him glory. Then one of the angels spoke to us and said, 'A child is born in Bethlehem which is Christ the Lord; the Son of God. Go see. He is lying in a manger dressed in swaddling clothes. Give praise to God in the Highest.' Then he ascended up to heaven. We left our sheep and came right away by following the star."

"Come see the child."

As they looked at the babe lying in the manger, they knelt in the attitude of prayer. When they turned around there were tears streaming down their faces. They smiled at Joseph and then at Mary and turned and walked out the opening to the stable, with reverence and with awe without saying another word.

☙◦❧

"I cannot understand it. I was sure Joseph and Mary would be here today. Where can they be?" Mary Elizabeth questioned.

"Maybe Joseph decided to let Mary rest another day. We will look for them tomorrow."

"I wonder if the baby has been born. If that were the case, Mary would not be able to be moved for a while. That would make them even later", Mary Elizabeth explained. "I knew I should have stayed with them."

"Come on, Mary Elizabeth, let us go see if the star leads to the Christ Child."

They walked to the edge of town. The star definitely rested on the stable behind the Inn. As they came near, they could see a faint light inside the building.

The two of them stood by the entrance and peered in.

They were surprised when the people inside were Joseph and Mary. They were not the ones they had expected to see. Actually, they did not know who they would see, but it definitely was not Joseph and Mary.

"Joseph, Mary, what are you doing here?" Mary Elizabeth asked. "Where is the Holy Child? We came because of the star." Joseph pointed to the manger.

"Is that your baby?" John queried.

"No, it is God's Holy Child", was all Joseph could say. His voice choked up and tears came to his eyes.

Mary Elizabeth looked puzzled. "But where is *your* baby?"

Joseph again pointed to the manger, "It is he."

Startled, Mary Elizabeth and John walked to the baby's bed and looked. The baby slept.

Mary Elizabeth started crying, "Why did I not know? I should have known. How long have you known?"

Mary beckoned the woman to come to her.

She walked reverently to the mother and sat down beside her.

"Ever since I conceived. An angel came to me one night and told me that I was to be the 'Chosen One'. He then went to Joseph and told him. That is why we were married so soon."

"Why did you not tell me?" Mary Elizabeth asked disappointedly.

"Both of us were told not to tell anyone. You know if I could have told anyone, I would have told you. You *are* my best friend. I just could not. Even our parents do not know."

"Why were you not allowed to tell anyone?" John questioned.

"I am not sure. Maybe because of the notoriety. Maybe because no one would believe it and think it was blasphemy. I really do not know. All I really do know is that we were told not to tell anyone", Mary stated.

Mary Elizabeth put her arms snuggly around Mary's shoulder and said, "I am really glad it is you."

She then went again and looked at the baby. "May I hold him?"

"Of course you can."

Mary Elizabeth picked up the child and looked adoringly at his face. As she looked at Mary, the tears ran down her cheeks. She had seen the Christ Child.

ॐ∘ॐ

The story of Joseph's and Mary's arrival into Bethlehem and the birth of Jesus Christ is found in the New Testament KJV Luke 2:4-21

CPSIA information can be obtained
at www.ICGtesting.com
Printed in the USA
LVHW102219261022
731683LV00024B/538